Prisoners of the Fugitive

Conant cried out in pain, and pain woke him as he sprawled on his right side. He looked upward and saw old Casper's face registering triumph, then disbelief, then horror, all in the moment of Conant's fall; and there was Tony lunging across the table, hand snatching at the rifle. Old Casper roared in terror and swung his club again . . .

Conant saw all—club, faces, fingers, eyes—as the lamp tipped slowly from the table and crashed to the floor, showering his cheek with flying splinters of glass. In that moment he responded instinctively, an animal fighting for life. He rolled beneath the table, escaping the second swipe of old Casper's club. He clawed at his Colt and reared upward under the table with a violence that surpassed theirs . . .

"Frank O'Rourke stands out among authors of sagebrush sagas . . . gifted and illuminating tale-telling."
—*Los Angeles Herald Examiner*

"A new O'Rourke is always cause for rejoicing."
—Luke Short

Books by Frank O'Rourke

Ambuscade
Blackwater
The Bravados
Desperate Rider
Gunsmoke Over Big Muddy
High Vengeance
Latigo
Legend in the Dust
The Professionals
Thunder in the Sun
Violence at Sundown
Warbonnet Law

Published by POCKET BOOKS

FRANK O'ROURKE

DESPERATE RIDER

POCKET BOOKS

New York   London   Toronto   Sydney   Tokyo

POCKET BOOKS, a division of Simon & Schuster Inc.
1230 Avenue of the Americas, New York, NY 10020

Published by arrangement with the author

ISBN: 0-671-66213-9

First Pocket Books printing April 1989

10 9 8 7 6 5 4 3 2 1

POCKET and colophon are trademarks of
Simon & Schuster Inc.

Printed in the U.S.A.

DESPERATE RIDER

-------------------- One --------------------

REALLY TO UNDERSTAND, YOU MUST SEE CONANT AS he existed in his world of that time. He was not an immoral man by the standards of New Mexico Territory, nor was he cruel in the sense of knowing cruelty. No, you must see in him something far worse: an ordinary human caught up in the most ordinary net of shoddy acts. He had gotten drunk and struck down a man of influence; he was brought to trial and given ten years for attempted murder; this, mind you, in a country of laughable legality where convicted murderers walked free after serving three years of life sentences. Conant had no influence. He served two years before he recognized the truth: He would serve ten full years for committing a misdemeanor. The desire to live in freedom is the oldest, strongest emotion; it can change any man. Conant escaped from Santa Fe Territorial Prison on the first of May, 1900, and escaping, killed two guards. He fled upriver with a hundred men on his trail.

He was thirty that spring, native of the upper river country, an Anglo fluent in Spanish and the ways of his land. Of medium height and build, he was an unprepossessing

7

figure with his typical rider's body, the sloping shoulders and long arms and strong, rope-burned hands, thin waist and narrow hips caging the little potgut just swelling under his belt. His legs were not muscled for walking: see him on the fourth morning of his freedom, crouching in the creek willows, feet bloody in his ruined boots.

He wore a blue cotton shirt and levis taken from a fruit farmer near Espanola; his faded yellow straw hat with unraveled brim had been lifted from the Taos Junction depot. He had a .94 Winchester and .38 Colt, former property of the Territory. He carried the cartridges in his hip pockets which bulged like a squirrel's cheeks during nuttime. He had stolen a horse in Santa Fe and ridden it to death between Taos Junction and the river; from there he had walked into the deep gorge and upriver, hiding by day, until he reached the mouth of Taos Creek and left the Rio Grande. He reasoned shrewdly that posses might look closer up Taos Canyon and over Mora Pass because he had worked the outfits in Moreno Valley and along the eastern slopes. He was starved and desperate that morning, knowing instinctively he must find a hole and vanish, gain time while the pursuit spread. He was five miles from Taos, and the last farm, just ahead on the south bank, was far downstream from its nearest neighbor. Watching, he saw the girl come from the house and descend the path with her water pail.

"Now or never!" Conant said aloud.

Old Casper cared only to sit at home and meditate on a life three-quarters spent, drink wine and smoke Bull Durham, the sack and papers forever on the bench beside him. He sat in the sun now with summer not yet come, but in the hot months he followed the shade. His daughter-in-law came from the house with the water bucket and he snorted

8

contemptuously as she passed with downcast face. His son had gone to town for supplies and some drinking talk with friends, and because his son was happy today old Casper did not heckle her with his usual cruelty.

His anger was the ignorant buckshot of a scattergun, the never-ending reference to her bad leg, the fact that she could not bear children by his fine, strong son. He wanted a grandson in his own image, a boy even better than his son, and she would not produce. He hated her, and beyond that, unrealizing, hated himself far more. He called her a failure and blotted out the greater truth: that in all his sixty-three years he had done nothing worthwhile. He came into the country when opportunity almost knocked a man down and stuffed his pockets with success. He married a Pina girl in '69, expecting a fat share of Pina's estate, but Pina grew to know him far too well. Pina willed them the farm and one thousand in gold.

That was hugely generous for any man but Casper felt himself betrayed. Not only in patrimony but beneath the yoke of bloodlines. His first name was Anthony and when his son was born her family changed it to Antonio over his protests. Young Tony was half gringo and half Spanish, but all Spanish as he grew. He blossomed while Casper spent the gold and sold off pieces of the pasture land until only the creek-bottom fields remained. Young Tony accepted his heritage merrily. He worked to eat and dress well, jingle spending money in his pocket. When the mother died twelve years ago, old Casper was relieved. The last gentle thorn had departed his conscience. They had the place to themselves. He evolved great plans but he ended here, on the creek farm, a widower with one son and a crippled daughter-in-law, an old man soured in his own juice.

"No-good bitch," he said. "Can't do nothin' right!"

* * *

The girl walked slowly, favoring her bad leg, the toe dragging below the stiff knee. She had broken her leg on the cliff across the creek one month after her marriage when, still bubbling with youth, she climbed to catch the wind, the freedom that had no name. She lost her footing, fell, and struck a rock. They wagoned her into town and the doctor did his whisky-soaked best, but there was no chance. She was a living symbol of her kind, bowing to fate, accepting bad luck; but no matter her fatalism, she was not a coward. Wearing no shoes in the house, her foot made a gentle sound on the dirt floor, as gentle as she was in all her ways. Beneath tousled black hair, brown eyes were set wide in the brown face. The red mouth was too soft and yielding, proof of her character: to give, never to take. But her jaw was strong as if solidness lay dormant, waiting until she found the courage to demand.

She knelt on the flat rock, filled her bucket, and returned to the house where her life was spent with a husband who no longer loved and a father-in-law who hated.

"Hurry it up," old Casper growled.

"Yes, Father," she said.

"Beans, beans, beans," old Casper said. "Well, get on with it!"

She started coffee and fed little gnarled chunks of piñon into the cookstove firebox under the beanpot. Old Casper shifted on his pine bench and stared blankly at high peaks and deep blue sky. Surrounded by majesty, he saw only the dusty yard and animals and conical mounds of dried manure. When the cooking smell twitched his long, red nose he went inside and sat at the round oak table. The girl brought his plate, poured his coffee, and retreated silently to the stove.

"Where's the sugar?" old Casper asked.

"We have none," Rachel Casper said meekly.

"You tell Tony?"

"Yes, Father."

"Helluva note," old Casper said, "when a man has to buy the groceries. Why don't you go to town?"

"I have much work, Father."

"Hah, work!" old Casper said, staring pointedly at her bad leg.

Tony Casper stood at the Columbian bar with his friends, drinking wine, acquiring that tipsy feeling of magnitude. Hat pushed up on jet black hair, accentuating his narrow, handsome face in which his mother's blood dominated, he laughed uproariously at a joke and lifted his glass. This was his element—the cheap bar, the cheap wine, the friendless friends. He was twenty-eight that spring, married three years and already roaming the valley from Ranchos to Arroyo Hondo in search of agreeable women who walked straight and did not stare with sad eyes. He accepted his wife's failure to produce children and, quite logically from his viewpoint, ceased treating her as a woman. What did it matter? She washed and cooked, life went on, there were other women. He was happy. He drank—and a deputy came from the courthouse with the latest news of the escaped murderer.

"Eh," Tony Casper said. "What's all this, Carlos?"

The deputy told of Conant's escape, how he killed two guards and ran upriver, how they trailed him through Ojo Caliente to Taos Junction and found his dead horse half-way to the river crossing. The telegraph wires had strummed, sending orders to Raton, Springer, Las Vegas; posses were guarding all the eastern passes because Conant had worked in Moreno Valley and around Cimarron.

"How long had he served?" Tony asked.

11

"Two years."

"For attempted murder?"

"For a misdemeanor," the deputy laughed cynically. "I can sympathize with him."

"Who did he assault?" Tony said.

"An important man from Springer," the deputy said. "He could not get parole. They say he will not be taken alive, that he could no longer face prison life."

"Bah!" Tony said. "His kind are cowards at heart."

"Lion or coward," the deputy said, "there is one thousand dollars reward, dead or alive."

"Then let him visit us," Tony said gaily. "We'll handle him, me and the old man."

"Your old man knew them all in those days, eh?" someone said. "Allison . . . the Kid?"

"He did," Tony said proudly. "Let me tell you . . ."

Conant followed the path up the bluff into the yard and flattened against the house wall. He heard one man eating, talking, and guessed the girl's position near the stove. The smell of food was overpowering; it was this place or nothing. He slipped around the casing and appeared in the doorway, centering the Winchester muzzle on the old man at the table.

"You," Conant said. "Hands up. . . . You there."

"Yes, señor," she said.

"Anybody else live here?"

"My husband Antonio, señor. He is in town."

"When's he due back?"

"I cannot say," she said. "Tonight perhaps."

"Feed me," Conant said. "You . . . stand up!"

Old Casper was atrophied, tongue, mind, and body, by the reincarnation of the past when such wild men came from nowhere into the villages and lonely camps. Starved, ragged, dirty, but always carrying clean weapons and big knives sharp as sin. Old Casper rose from his chair and awaited the shot, for these men were invariably crazy.

"Get over on that south wall," Conant said. "Stick your nose in a crack."

Old Casper ran to the wall and pushed his long nose into the cool adobe. Conant went to the table and took the chair facing the girl and old man.

"You can turn around," he said. "Let your hands down."

Old Casper turned fearfully and saw the crazy man eating with left hand, Colt in right, rifle across his knees.

"You ain't goin' to shoot?" old Casper gasped.

"Not if you be good."

"We got no money, mister."

"You," Conant said. "Bring that beanpot here."

Rachel Casper brought the beanpot and backed away. Conant pushed Casper's plate aside and ate directly from the pot, plying his spoon like a pitchfork. That sight was reassuring to old Casper. When Conant pushed away and fished at his shirt pocket, old Casper spoke eagerly.

"I got the makings. . . . Can I reach?"

"Go on," Conant said.

Old Casper tossed his sack and papers to the table. Conant's right hand shifted the Colt to his left, then worked expertly, forming the cigarette, scratching a match, squeezing the brown paper as his lungs drew smoke. Old Casper breathed easier. This was no ghost from the past, no crazy man, but a banty-assed cowhand down on his luck . . . oh, something more, of course, being half-starved and plainly on the run.

"You in trouble?" he asked.

"Shut up," Conant said. "Don't you two move."

They stood mutely while he searched the big room. He

found the rifle and shotgun, smashed off the hammers, carried all knives and the axe to the corner behind the table. Then he nodded toward the inner doorway.

"Whose room?"

"Mine," Old Casper said. "My son's."

"And her?"

Old Casper pointed to the cot against the north wall. Conant ripped the blankets off, inspected the rawhide webbing that served as mattress and springs, and faced the inner doorway.

"Both of you, hands up, go in ahead of me."

Inside, he faced them against the west wall and tore the room apart. He emptied the shelves and dresser, found a sheath knife and a little .32 caliber banker's special. He thrust that into his belt, pocketed the cartridges, and marched them back into the big room.

"Now squat down," he said. "Cross your legs."

Old Casper dropped like a shot and huddled into the wall, but the girl went down slowly and could not bend her bad leg. Conant saw the pain and said gruffly, "Never mind," and moved over beside the front door and looked upstream. "Who lives up there?"

"Gonzales," old Casper said.

"He come down here much?"

"Nossir," old Casper said. "Hardly ever."

Conant carried a chair to the doorway and seated himself in the shadows facing them and the outdoors. He laid the Winchester across his thighs as he tilted back against the wall and sighed gustily with the bloody ache in his feet.

"I want no trouble," he said. "I'm staying here awhile so make the best of it. When your son comes home, we'll figure ways and means . . . savvy?"

"I don't want no trouble," old Casper agreed quickly.

"You ain't done nothin' to us, I'll not hinder you. . . . I reckon you're wanted, mister?"

"You might say it's unanimous," Conant said dryly.

"You, what grub you got?"

"Beans," Rachel Casper said. "Some ham, there are chickens—"

"Outside," Conant said softly, "and we stay inside. You take that butcher knife, cut off a big piece of ham, start that with some more beans and coffee. I'm so damn hungry I'll never plug the gap. . . . Old man, you got a watch?"

Casper fumbled the repeater from his vest. "Eight minutes of eleven."

"What's he riding?" Conant asked.

"My son? . . . A black with a star."

"You better hope he's alone," Conant said.

He sat back, face gray beneath the ragged straw hat, rolling another cigarette. He smoked and watched them and watched the trail winding upstream beside the creek, the Winchester lax beneath his fingers on his thighs. The girl sliced ham and started the beanpot, fed the fire, worked silently over the stove, sweat beading her face and spreading dark beneath her arms in the worn folds of her cotton dress. Conant rested for the first time in five days and nights, but rest did not include eyes and mind and senses, only muscle and bone and bloody feet. He gave them no consideration as people, faces, individuals; there was too much facing him at nightfall. The son must be handled quietly, their routine learned and shaped to remain natural, his bodily needs assuaged. He needed three specific elements: food and rest, time, and a good horse. He sat in the chair, smoking, while time scarcely moved.

"How long you goin' to stay here?" old Casper asked.

"Old man," Conant said wearily, "lay down on your belly and shut your mouth. When your son comes home, I want it dead still in here, otherwise you get shot for practically no reason at all. That goes for you too, girl. Now shut up and wait!"

Two

FROM THE WEST, CREEPING SLOWLY, SUNSET SHADOW blurred the clean-edged willow branches murmuring in evening wind.

"Light that lamp," Conant said.

When yellow light fluttered timidly against encroaching darkness, the girl sensed vibration in the smoked glass and turned her great brown eyes to the east. Sound grew, distant hammers tapping the earth, a big horse running the creek trail that hugged the willows and splashed through soggy bottoms into the yard. The rider unsaddled, turned his horse into the corral, and came whistling toward the house, grocery sack swinging on his arm.

"Ho, Father!" he cried gaily. "I've got exciting news!"

A strong wine smell preceded him through the doorway. He saw old Casper on the floor and his mouth shaped words of surprise. Conant's rifle barrel sent him sprawling in a rubbery tangle of torso and limbs. The rifle covered old Casper, the girl was held within Conant's periphery as the son rolled over in outraged pain. Conant shut the door and dropped the bar in place.

"Stay there," he said. "You, dump that sack on the table."

Rachel Casper upended the flour sack; out tumbled coffee, sugar, tobacco, a black-skinned ham. No weapons, nothing dangerous. Behind her, the beanpot hissed and exuded a scorched smell. She said anxiously, "The beans, señor."

"Go ahead."

Tony Casper shook his addled head and stared at the man across the room. All afternoon he had told proudly of his father's exploits in the old days, how they would capture the murderer if he foolishly approached their farm. Here was his father groveling on the floor; here was the unbelievable holding a rifle, eyes shining through grime and beard.

"Conant!" he whispered.

"Guilty," Conant said. "What's the talk in town?"

"Of you?"

"Not you," Conant said harshly. "Speak up!"

"You are wanted," Tony Casper said. "Many officers are in town."

"What do they say?"

"You are near and they will find you."

"Where?"

"To the east," Tony said quickly.

"What's the reward?"

"One thousand dollars."

"One—!" old Casper said.

"Makes me a valuable man," Conant said, "and gives you ideas. Go on, think all you want, just don't get reckless."

But warning them, he saw the glint, the gleam, and knew that greed would conquer fear until they learned a bitter truth: Greed could not defeat lead.

"Don't worry," old Casper said. "We won't try nothin'!"

"Be still," Conant said absently.

He considered the black horse in the corral and the urge was overpowering: to take food and drink, ride westward in the protective night. He had rested; if he could treat his bloody feet, change boots . . . he looked at Tony Casper.

"What size boot you wear?"

"Eight."

Conant wore size six but two pair of socks would take up slack. "Kick 'em off."

Tony began pushing one toe against the other heel and glared petulantly at the girl. "Rachel—!"

"Do your own work," Conant said. "You, old man."

"Yessir."

"See that lariat rope on the peg?"

"Yessir."

"Get that rope, keep it behind you, step over by Tony . . . Tony, roll on your belly."

"But—"

"I'll tell you just once . . ." Conant said. "That's better. Well, old man!"

Old Casper rose and walked eggshell soft to the peg and took down the coiled lariat rope. He returned to his son and stared helplessly at Conant.

"Push out your toes, Tony," Conant said. "Swing both arms in the small of your back. Old man, tie his legs above and below the ankles, run your rope to his wrists and tie them."

Old Casper knelt and looped the rope around his son's ankles; as he progressed to the wrists, wrapping and tying, he turned his back on Conant and murmured softly in Spanish. Conant heard disconnected snatches of those

19

warning words but gave no sign he understood, even when old Casper called him a foul name.

"Leave a ten-foot dangle," he said. "Cut it off."

He tossed the butcher knife from the table and old Casper measured two armlengths and sawed the rope apart.

"Now toss it back."

Old Casper rose creakily and revolved the knife handle in his palm; it lay point down in throwing position and the desire made his fat shoulders quiver. The rifle lifted an inch, centering on his chest. He tossed the knife onto the table and coiled the remaining rope, his hands trembling over the smooth hemp.

"Squat down," Conant said. "You . . . Rachel."

"Yes, señor."

"Put on a bucket of water, then bring me Tony's boots."

He placed his chair against the east wall, facing them, and watched her put water on the stove and bring the boots.

"You got clean socks?" he said. "Salve?"

"Yes, señor."

"Get me that salve and all the socks."

"In the bedroom?"

"Go on!"

He met her gaze for a moment. Spirit flickered and subsided before she turned and walked slowly past her husband into the bedroom. He heard her rummage through drawers and saw fresh hope touch old Casper's eyes.

"Window's too small," Conant said. "No cigar, old man."

But that hope clung until the girl returned with socks and a can of ointment; then bitter disappointment clouded old Casper's eyes as though the girl had betrayed him.

"How's the water?" Conant asked.

"Warm, señor."

"Bring it here," Conant said. "Then go over on your bed."

He sat with the bucket between his feet, feeling heat rise moist over his face. Watching them, he placed the rifle on the table, laid his Colt beside it; lifting one leg, he drew off the boot and peeled the tattered sock from his foot. Old Casper's eyes widened with pleasure at sight of such bloody pain, watched Conant bare his other foot and lower both into the bucket.

"I'll live, old man," he said.

"Yessir."

Conant soaked his feet until the water cooled, dried them gently on a sock, smeared the broken blisters and purple stone bruises with salve. He drew on two pair of socks and tensed himself for the ordeal; but Tony's boots were loose. His feet slipped easily into place, and he stood erect in triumph.

"Rachel," he said, "you help the old man put Tony on his bed, face down."

They yanked and lifted until Tony Casper lay in the center of the bed. Conant tossed rope and butcher knife to old Casper, motioned the girl against the wall.

"Cut off four lengths," he said. "Tie his hands and feet to the posts . . . and tight, old man, tight!"

Old Casper cut and tied, mumbling to himself, working in the bedroom gloom, his eyes straying toward some invisible spot Conant had missed in his previous search.

"I'm backing out," Conant said. "Both of you follow. Bring the rope and knife."

He led them into the big room, waited until the knife clattered on the table, and thumbed old Casper to the floor.

"Let's see," he said. "About twenty feet of rope left. Rachel, tie him up like he tied Tony."

"Aw, now—" old Casper whined.

"Shut up . . . roll over!"

He stood in line with the inner doorway, watching the man on the bed while Rachel Casper tied the old man so tightly he resembled a fat boat with high prows.

"Now bring the lamp," Conant ordered.

He marched her into the bedroom and spoke quietly to them all: "Where is it?"

Silence answered him, great waves of outraged innocence from both men, protesting such an unfair question. Old Casper groaned and Tony's visible eye rolled in bewilderment.

"Well," Conant said, "the dresser's over there on the north wall. When you got the socks, Rachel, the old man jiggled like tapioca pudding. But gun or knife, it wasn't in the dresser so it must be hard to reach. . . . Stand there!"

He pulled the dresser from the wall; but the adobes were smooth with cobwebs and dust. He looked upward at the vegas, heavy lengths of pine adzed to rough squareness. He could touch the beams with his left hand and he felt along the junction of vega and ceiling mat in the thick shadows . . . one vega, another, and his fingers explored the hollow between vega and ceiling mat, rubbed the oily slick steel. He pulled the Winchester carbine from its hiding place, another gun identical with his own.

"Go out," he said.

He followed her into the big room and took his chair beside the table. "Get away from the lamp," he said. "Back on your cot."

"Yes, señor."

Conant laid his Winchester on the table, and hefted the hideout carbine. He unloaded the magazine, lowered the hammer, and looked at the old man.

"What you goin' to do?" old Casper asked.

"You stole it," Conant said. "Otherwise you wouldn't hide it out . . . didn't you?"

"No," old Casper said emphatically. "Let me tell you—"

"No matter."

Conant worked the lever, clubbed the rifle, and smashed the hammer against the doorpost. The stock splintered and the breech jumped from its cutout. Conant tossed the useless rifle into the corner and faced them.

"Now listen," he said. "First I want to eat. Then I've got to tie you up, Rachel. I'll sack grub, borrow the horse, and say so long. . . . Tony, what's the black worth?"

"One hundred dollars," Tony called.

"I'll send you fifty," Conant said. "More if he's worth your price."

"Ahhh!" Tony Casper groaned. *"Caballejo!"*

"Talk American," Conant said.

"My horse," Tony said. "He is everything to me."

"Want me to take your wife?" Conant asked sharply. "Or don't she count? . . . Rachel, bring me that food."

She served the meal and Conant ate until the spoon clogged his mouth. He swept groceries into the flour sack with frying pan, pot, and butcher knife, tied the string and dropped it beside his chair.

"Get on the cot," he said. "Ill tie you good, but one of you three ought to work loose by morning. If you can't, live off your hump."

"There is no more rope, señor."

"Then rip a blanket," Conant said. "Here, take the knife."

But extending one hand, her head tilted suddenly in alertness, brought to life by the faint tapping of far-off hoofs. Conant leaped to the door, lifted the bar, threw it open in the natural position. He pushed all evidence of his presence—ruined boots, socks, gear—behind the table. He caught old Casper's collar and dragged him into the bedroom; many horses were near, bunched on the creek trail, and one horse ascended the path into the yard.

"Old man," Conant said, "you and Tony get the first shots. . . . Rachel, get rid of them, don't let anybody inside."

"Yes, señor."

Old Casper groaned and Tony was silent. Conant stood beside the bed in darkness, rifle up, as the horse stopped and the rider hailed the house.

"Ho in there . . . anybody up?"

Conant watched her move into the doorway, answer the unseen man in her gentle voice. His breath seemed loud in his throat; he swallowed thickly as Rachel Casper spoke with the man, explaining that her father-in-law was asleep, her husband in bed and not feeling well. . . . The unseen man laughed coarsely and mentioned too much wine, then asked if she had seen or heard a stranger during the day. She denied that and the rider warned her to be alert for the escaped murderer named Conant, somewhere in the valley now. They were going to patrol the river from the Tres Piedras ford to the Taos Junction bridge.

"Thanks, girl," the rider said. "Good night."

"Buenas noches, señor," she replied softly.

The horse trotted from the yard, the rider called, hoofs struck and diminished in the night as the posse rode downstream toward the river.

"Close the door," Conant said.

She dropped the bar and turned, her face expressionless in the lamplight. Conant leaned over the bed and slapped Tony Casper's face viciously.

"Where are they watching?" he said. "To the east . . . !

You bastard, ten minutes more and I'd be in the soup.''

"But they told me—"

"What I just heard," Conant said. "Well, that settles it!"

"What?" old Casper said fearfully.

"Stay here till they ease off," Conant said, talking to himself, not to them, as he pulled old Casper from the bedroom and resumed his seat against the wall. "East is closed off for sure, can't go north or south, and now the river's too hot." He cradled the rifle across his thighs and stared at old Casper. "Are you ready to give me straight answers now?"

"Yessir," old Casper said thinly.

"Two lies," Conant said. "The rifle, now this. . . . That's your limit, old man, you and Don Juan in there. I don't want to stay here any more than you want me. But I stay till they loosen up along the river or east in the passes. Is anybody due here for three or four days?"

"Not a soul!" old Casper said.

"Tony?"

"Believe me," Tony Casper said fervently. "No one!"

"Rachel," Conant said. "You tell me . . . and tell me, knowing what happens to them if you lie."

"No one comes here, señor."

"These two expected anywhere, to work for somebody?"

"I do not know, señor."

"Old man?"

"In four days," old Casper said. "We promised Webber—"

"Where does he live?"

"East of Ranchos church."

"That would be Saturday?" Conant said.

"Yessir, in the morning. He's making up a batch."

"Whisky?"

"Yessir."

"That adds up," Conant said. "You'd be the one to help. . . . Got anything to tell me, Tony?"

"It is true," Tony Casper said. "I swear it!"

"Rachel, unpack the groceries," Conant said. "Wash your dishes, do whatever you do before bedtime."

"Yes, señor."

"And take your time," Conant said. "We'll have a god's plenty before Friday night rolls round."

"You goin' to try it then?" Old Casper asked.

"Have to," Conant said. "If they don't ease up in the four days, they never will."

"Then you won't shoot us?"

"I don't want to shoot anybody," Conant said. "Just be good and we'll work it out some way. Now there's things to plan, the proper way to do them. Tony, can your black horse get to feed?"

"In the shed."

"I'll feed him night and morning," Conant said. "Rachel, how many meals you cook a day?"

"Three, señor."

"Then we eat three," Conant said. "How about wood?"

"Behind the house, señor."

"Water?"

"From the creek."

"No well," Conant said disgustedly. "Fine menfolks you got. . . . We'll handle that. You'll stay tied except to eat and—" he looked meaningly at old Casper. "Where is it?"

"Out back."

"Which way?"

"A hundred foot west."

"All right," Conant said. "I'll take you one at a time, right after dark and before sunup. Regulate yourselves accordingly."

"I—" old Casper said desperately.

"In due time," Conant snapped. "Rachel, do your housework."

The dishes were washed, the floor swept, fresh coffee boiled on the stove; the coal oil lamp guttered as the tank burned low around the curling wick. Old Casper lay on his side and watched Conant tie Rachel, enter the bedroom, march Tony through the house into the night. When their steps died away old Casper hissed.

"Can you get loose?"

"There is no time, Father."

"Oh , the hell with you!" old Casper said. "Might of known you'd be no help."

He gazed longingly at the weapons behind the table and thought of the reward. Conant returned with Tony, retied him, and took Rachel into the night. Tony whispered despondently from the bedroom.

"Father, I can't get loose."

"I can," old Casper said.

"What!"

"But not in five minutes."

"What will we do? . . . Father, we must do something!"

"Patience," old Casper soothed. "Don't try to jump the gun. We'll get him."

"Hist!"

"Bueno."

They lay innocently when Conant returned, tied Rachel, and loosened old Casper's ropes. Casper was silent during

27

his walk in the clear, sweet night air; nor did he speak when they returned and Conant lashed him down for the night. He watched Conant untie Rachel again, order her to pour coffee, fill the lamp, set the coal oil can beside the table. Cramped and aching, old Casper hunched himself around until he faced Conant.

"Care if I talk?"

"Talk your head off," Conant said.

"I can't sleep," old Casper said. "Not yet anyway."

"You will."

"I reckon," old Casper said mournfully. "Say, how come they want you so bad?"

"You heard the man."

"He didn't say much," old Casper said. "Called you a killer . . . ?"

"Guess so."

"You must of killed a guard," old Casper prompted.

"Two."

"Glory be!" old Casper said in awed tones. "You sure are from the wild bunch. . . . Did you know Allison and the Kid?"

"How the hell could I?" Conant said. "I was sucking a sugartit when they were around."

"I knew them all," old Casper said proudly, as if Conant had neither affirmed nor denied association. "I saw the Kid three times, I worked for Clay at Cimarron . . . you hear about the time Clay shot them buffalo soldiers in Lambert's saloon?"

"Yes," Conant said.

"Well," old Casper said momentously, "I was there!"

"You make five hundred and one," Conant said.

"What?"

"Witnesses," Conant said. "I've been in Lambert's. It'll hold fifty at most."

28

Conant stared morosely at his hands but old Casper talked on as though he faced an admiring audience. His words meant nothing to Conant. He was no gunman, he had no truck with that vanished race. Old Casper was lying but his need was obvious: He had to offer something out of his past to stand comparison with Conant's record. He peered enviously at Conant, the relict, throwback to the days when Casper was forever on the outside, nose against the candy store window, watching the big boys roister within. Old Casper droned on and, in his meandering, took on solid shape and substance in Conant's eyes. He would soon know them all, they would know him. It was nothing to be desired. He thought of sleep and tomorrow, all the vague, questionable tomorrows, until the old man ran down like a dollar watch and the girl was nodding on her cot.

"You sleepy?" Conant asked.

"Yes, señor."

"Got to tie you," he said.

He walked to the cot where she was already turning face downward. He tested the strips of ripped blankets and examined the cot closely: Built of solid timbers, nailed into the wall and floor, it was a crude affair. She slept here while they had the bed with spring and mattress.

"You can lay on your back," Conant said.

"No matter, señor."

"Turn up," Conant said gruffly.

When she rolled over painfully, he tied her ankles to the corner posts. She winced as his hand accidentally struck her bad leg.

"Sorry," he said.

"It was nothing, señor."

He bent far over, tying her wrists, and looked closely into her face. He saw it in minute detail, eyes and cheeks and soft red mouth, tiny wrinkles around the great brown

29

eyes, flecks of dirt embedded in the forehead pores beneath the black hair. He had lived two years in prison; she was the first woman he had touched in that time. He grunted, tying the wrist strips to give her a few inches play if she had to brush her face. She stared upward calmly, unseeing, accepting without passion or protest. She was unnatural to Conant; no woman in all his narrow experience had behaved in this way.

"Does the leg bother you much?" he asked.

"No, señor."

"But you limp," he said accusingly. "You can't bend the knee."

"Enough, señor."

Her patience worried him, brought harsh words that relieved his own impatience.

"Unhandy," he said. "Doing some things."

"I would not know."

"Why not?" he asked.

"I do few things, señor."

"You're married."

"Yes."

"How long?" Conant asked.

"Three years in June."

"And no kids?"

"No, señor."

"And it don't bother you?" he said cruelly. "The hell it don't!"

She had infinite patience, something Conant could not understand. She looked upward, her face unmoving, until he turned away in disgust. He knew old Casper had listened and he wondered what they'd say if he took the girl outside . . . but he knew that too. Nothing, not a damned thing, not the way they treated her.

"No spunk," he muttered. "No nothin'."

* * *

Life was very lonely for Rachel Casper. After her leg healed and she could walk, and work, Tony came to her again, but with one purpose: to get her with child. When time passed and she showed no sign, he stopped. But he had stopped long before in truth; the body could make the movements of love and lie. She was left alone. She had been alone for nearly three years.

She held the peyote buttons in her clenched left hand while Conant tied her. She had taken six from her secret cubby behind the stove; now, watching him toe off her husband's boots and pad about the room, she moved her bound hands to her mouth and took one bitter green button. She chewed slowly, tasting the bitterness, shutting off the room from her thoughts. She took the peyote only on those nights when all had gone wrong during the day; it was her secret, kept from others for two years.

When they went away at night, as they so often did, and time went on dying with each breath, she talked to the walls and the sky. Understanding seemed to move between them. She lay in her bed and dreamed, for that was her only private happiness. She dreamed no vision of overpowering her father-in-law, healing her bad leg, winning back her husband's lost love. Those were facts you woke to. No, she dreamed of nothing and all, for in her sleep was freedom. She shared it with no one; it was hers alone and she was rich. And through the worst nights she ate peyote and the dreams took on more color and sweetness; she floated happily until morning and woke clearheaded to face another empty, loveless day.

The first button was gone and she chewed the second, eating faster than her friend, the old Ute, recommended; but tonight she desired oblivion quickly. She chewed and

31

the colors brightened against the film of her closed eyelids, she began to float and smile, she left the room and entered her dreams.

Conant soaped his face and shaved with old Casper's razor, baring his wind-burned skin in the warped mirror. He saw a gaunt, cold-eyed face and marveled at the change in five short days . . . but that was not true. Change had begun the day he entered prison; he had become a different man through the merciless passage of seven hundred days. Perhaps the old man did compare him rightfully with those tarnished names: Clay Allison, the Kid, that race of vanished men.

"Hell!" he said.

He dried his smarting face and went to the bedroom door. Tony Casper lay spread-eagled, breathing gustily through his long, thin nose. Conant turned and studied old Casper who slept noisily, emitting grunts and whistles, or imitated sleep so perfectly he could not tell the difference. He guessed that old Casper had sharp ears, woke instantly to alien sound, was probably a cat in darkness.

He settled in the chair and pulled the holster forward between his thighs. The watch ticked off the hours . . . ten-thirty now . . . he dared not sleep past four. Light came early in May, he must do the chores and be inside by then. Conant leaned his head on folded arms, let weariness claim an overdue toll.

"Father!"

Old Casper replied so softly his mouth scarcely moved; his tongue released the answer in Spanish.

"Wait!"

He observed Conant another minute, just as he had watched for two hours. Then he rolled slowly and inched himself across the floor to the limit of the rope Conant had tied to a window casing post. Facing the bedroom door he could speak, not in whispers that carried dangerously, but in the soft Spanish that lent itself to shadows and intrigue.

"He sleeps."

"Father, can you get loose?"

"What about you?"

"Impossible."

"Your wrists?"

"Some play."

"Can you bend your fingers, touch the knots?"

"Barely . . . shall I try?"

"No . . . wait!"

Old Casper had been thinking for hours. He was a rank coward, his mind fat from years of disuse, but he was still an individualist; and above all he must play the bravo before his son if it killed him. All the years he told of his part in those heroic days . . . his son would detest him now if he did not play the role.

He had some qualities that were constant: He was a great liar, therefore he retained imagination. He was a good hater; he cursed government and religion and wealth with savage conviction. But these were not enough to effect a transformation for, in all truth, when an uncourageous man tried to rekindle himself he only spoke to his own conscience and claimed a brief thimbleful of courage. Tonight he needed more. He cursed Conant with great ferocity and lashed his cupidity with dreams of the reward. That was the best way: to create a burning desire for the money.

It was easy to wave aside a thousand dollars, be noble or generous as the case existed, but old Casper reduced the problem to a common denominator. When you and one son earned three hundred dollars a year at most, and saved fifty with luck, simple arithmetic proved that you needed twenty years to save one thousand dollars. Then the sum grew, meant something, became a matter of time . . . time you spent to save that much: twenty years! But on the other hand, if you were smart, ten seconds!

"Listen," old Casper said. "We can do it."

"How—?"

"You remember the can out back, on the eave above the door?"

"Yes."

"Filled with soap," old Casper said. "She leaves it there for scrubbing . . . by God, she does one thing that counts."

"Ah . . . !"

"Our hands are free when we go inside. You're taller, son, you can reach it easier. Do nothing tonight, maybe nothing tomorrow night unless I give the word. But when the time comes you must help me—"

"But how?"

"He must take her first, then you. We can work that. When you go in, take the can down for me. When I go in I can put soap in my mouth—not on my wrists or hands, he can feel and smell it—and bring it back into the house. After he falls asleep I'll soap my wrists, the rope and knots—"

"But your hands are tied behind your back, Father."

"I'll fix that," old Casper said. "It will work."

"Why wait?" Tony said eagerly. "In the morning, Father!"

"Fool!" old Casper said. "He is tired tonight. We must groan, keep waking him, spoil his sleep. During the day we can sleep in turn and wake each other. Get him so damn tired he'll drop off like a poleaxed cow. Then we'll have our chance."

"Tomorrow night?"

"I'll see," old Casper said. "Now wait till I move back. Then you start groaning, have bad dreams."

"*Bueno.*"

Old Casper rolled over and inched himself painfully to the wall. He lay exhausted, aching horribly, but filled with jubilation. He grinned at his own daring, his ingenuity. They could do it, by God, they could!

Conant leaped to his feet and tipped the chair backward against the wall. Tony Casper was threshing about, groaning loudly, rattling his bed. Conant ran to the door and saw the head bobbing, the mouth forming meaningless words.

"Dreaming," he said. "You . . . wake up!"

"Eh?"

He jabbed with the rifle. "Wake up!"

"What . . . what is wrong?"

"Stop dreaming," Conant said.

"I am sick," Tony Casper moaned. "I ache, my arms are filled with needles."

"Sew yourself!" Conant said.

He returned to the table and glanced at the watch: two o'clock. The girl was small and still in her corner, old Casper slept in a doglike ball. Conant righted the chair and resumed his seat; and it seemed he scarcely slept until more anguished groans woke him.

Old Casper was tangled in his rope, kicking futilely, calling for help from the depths of sleep. The watch read three o'clock when Conant kicked him soundly and man-handled him free of the tangle.

"What—?" old Casper asked.

"Can't you sleep decent?" Conant said.

"What was I doing?"

"Chasing rabbits," Conant said bitterly. "Ah, the hell with it!"

He dared not sleep now, an hour from first light, with the horse to feed, wood to carry, three people to manage. He drew on the boots and unbarred the door, half sick with the desire for sleep. He walked unsteadily to the shed and heard the black horse rubbing against the far wall. Conant moved cautiously in the darkness, spoke softly to the horse while his left hand located blankets, bridle, and saddle. He pulled hay into the manger and ladled out a double portion of oats; and stood beside the horse, searching for sores or flaws. And then he cursed aloud.

"No water!"

They had no trough or tank. They turned the horse into the pasture that bordered the creek; but if he took that chance would the horse return to feed? Was this black a roamer who chased the neighbor mares or crossed the creek and grazed high above the cliff? Conant hurried to the house and called sharply.

"Tony, will the black stay in your pasture?"

"Yes," Tony Casper said. "He is a good horse."

"He has to drink," Conant said. "If he gets away, you're done. . . . Now, can I turn him loose?"

"I swear it!" Tony said. "He has never run away."

"All right," Conant said softly. "We'll see."

He crossed the yard and opened the rickety gate in the corral fence. The black horse came from the shed, trotted through, and vanished down the path toward the creek. Conant found the woodpile and brought an armload inside. He made three trips to fill the box while they woke and watched him silently. Time was racing toward the dawn.

"Rachel," he said. "You're first."

She came unprotesting, moving in a daze, paying no

attention to wind or night or sky. When he retied her and approached the old man, Casper said, "Take my son first."

"Shut up," Conant said. "You go like I grab you."

He spent precious time on those slow journeys; and finally, both men retied, he left the house and wandered in the yard. He stared downward at the creek where the water shone dark. The black horse walked invisibly in the pasture; a trout splashed beneath the willows in the deep pool.

He was awake now, purified by the cold night wind. This was unchanged from all the days and nights of his flight. He had slept fitfully under the junipers at river edge in the gorge and marched at night with panic forever crowding; but wind and movement always cleared his head. Could he last until Friday night . . . and what of these people? He knew the truth: He was a dead man unless he got away. A persistent worry touched his thoughts, nagged him as he turned inside.

Three

MORNING MIST LIFTED FROM THE CREEK BOTTOM, MIXED smells flared richly on the wind, dry and sweet and rank, sage and wet grass, mud sucking where the cows had walked. He untied Rachel Casper and helped her stand erect.

"Douse the lamp," he said.

He watched the yellow flame give way to gray morning light touched with the acrid smell of coal oil smoke. She seemed awake, yet dreaming on her feet. Conant shook her arm.

"You sick?"

"No, señor."

"Better start the fire."

He stood in the doorway, facing eastward toward the shadowed hillfolds, the pastures, the deserted trail looping beside the creek.

"Got any eggs?" he asked.

"Only six, but there are more outside."

"Cook the six, with some ham," he said. "Fix up a plate for Tony first."

He moved restlessly to the south window and studied the rising slopes, empty green smudged with rock outcroppings, and now he felt the weight of his position in deadly earnest.

"Old man, anything south over the ridge?"

"Sheep graze," old Casper said.

"And north?"

"Same thing."

"I know this valley," Conant said. "There's farms north along that side creek."

"Oh sure," old Casper said innocently. "I thought you meant just over the rim."

"Go to sleep," Conant said wearily. "You'd lie to the Lord. Rachel, that grub ready?"

"Yes, señor."

"No fork or knife," he said. "One spoon . . . that's it . . . Now take it in on the dresser and untie Tony's hands and boost him up."

Tony Casper wrung his hands, rubbed them until he could hold the spoon. He ate with good appetite, drank his coffee in two gulps, and smiled at Conant.

"*Gracias* . . . another cup, eh?"

"No," Conant said. "Tie him up, Rachel."

She retied Tony's hands and when Conant checked the knots Tony closed his eyes. Conant laughed mirthlessly. "No need."

"Eh?"

"I know how you feel," Conant said. "Don't try to hide it."

"I ache," Tony said forlornly.

"No, you hate, and you'll hate me worse. All right, Rachel."

40

She returned to the stove, filled another plate and cup, and moved toward the old man.

"No," Conant said. "You eat that."

"But—"

"He got tricky," Conant said. "He don't eat till noon."

"Then you," she said meekly. "Men should eat first."

"Jesus Christ!" Conant exploded. "You're not a damn slave. Eat your meal!"

He stood fuming beside the door while she ate, drank her coffee, and filled his plate; and then she moved to her cot and sat, hands clasped, staring at the floor. Conant wolfed his food and drank three cups of coffee, coming fully awake with the force of his momentary anger that struck out blindly at the girl. The food gave him strength, coffee alerted him, but it was deceptive wakefulness. How much longer could he stay awake?

"Wash up," he said.

She washed the dishes, put the shelves to right, lifted the coffeepot questioningly. Conant nodded agreement and she spooned coffee from the grinder box.

"Go on," he said.

"Eight is proper, señor."

"Put in twelve," he said. "I don't want dishwater."

"Yes, señor."

Once the pot was bubbling, Conant tied her ankles and knotted the blanket end to a cotpost, leaving her hands free. "You can stay this way," he said, "if you're good."

"Thank you, señor."

Conant poured fresh coffee and arranged his position for the day. He laid the Winchester on the table and spent ten minutes cleaning the Colt, sipping coffee as he worked.

"Conant?" old Casper said.

41

"Yes."

"I deserved goin' hungry," old Casper said. "I ain't mad."

"You deserved more."

"Been the same story all my life," old Casper said humbly. "Stick out my neck, push my nose where it don't belong—"

"And get it smashed," Conant said.

"Plenty. . . . You mind if we talk?"

Conant faced the endless hours of the day. He must stay awake, inspect the surrounding country regularly, watch these people constantly. If the old man wanted to talk, it might be better than alarm clocks.

"Talk your head off," he said.

"Can I roll over?"

"Yes."

Old Casper turned and peered up at him owlishly. Conant prowled the room, looked at creek bottom and ridge, found a pencil stub, seated himself with a wrinkled piece of butcher paper. He was able, at last, to form a plan.

"You writing a letter?" old Casper asked.

"Sure," he said. "To the warden."

He looked at the west wall and beyond, saw the country flowing into the river gorge, the vast empty land to the west: sage and chamiso, piñon and juniper, pine forests offering cover and shelter, fire and food. Old Casper's voice prodded this privacy, light with companionable humor.

"I reckon he'd like that. Goin' to tell him where to reach you?"

"I'll draw him a map," Conant said.

The map was in his mind. He remembered Tres Piedras, huge gray rocks thrusting upward from the earth,

42

pines mounting the long slopes, game trails veining the forest beyond the railroad track that came from Santa Fe and lost itself northward in the direction of Alamosa. Cross the creek here, he thought, go northwest to the river, get through the gorge and beyond the tracks, then swing south for Mexico. He touched pencil to paper.

"How come you broke out?" old Casper said. "It's none of my business but I've had friends down there. They come home and told me how it was."

"How was it to them?" Conant asked incuriously.

One night to ride from here across the river and beyond the tracks. He had to make that run—thirty-odd miles—or be naked to all enemies at dawn.

". . . not fit for pigs," old Casper was saying. "Rotten food, bedbugs, blankets like tissue paper. And guards! . . . I don't need to tell you about them."

"No," Conant said. "I was on close speaking terms with the guards." He laughed shortly. "They spoke and I listened."

"I'd appreciate to hear," old Casper said hopefully.

"Hear what?"

"Well," old Casper said. "I've seen the prison. High walls, guards with rifles and shotguns and them Gatlings . . . I knew you killed two and got a clean start, but how in hell did you do it?"

"How would you try it?" Conant countered.

Once in the pine forest, he thought, he would move south, detour wide around Chama and El Rito, work down past Ojo Caliente and Frijoles—

"Me?" old Casper said. "Not knowing the inside setup, I can't guess. But I busted out of jail once—never mind where—that was thirty years ago—"

"Jail!" Conant said. "Jails are crackerboxes alongside Santa Fe."

"That's it," old Casper said quickly. "I wouldn't know where to start. You don't mean to tell me you busted from inside?"

"I've told you nothing," Conant said.

"I never meant to pry."

"Like hell," Conant said, "but it don't matter. I was outside. How do you get outside? I'll tell you, old man, in case you end up there. You get a number and a cell, you start sprouting wings you want to be so damn good and bother nobody, seeing as how you won't be in more'n fifteen months with good behavior. Little Lord Fauntleroy himself—"

"Who?"

"Don't you read?" Conant said. "Oh, forget it. I toed the chalk line, took the dirt, caused no trouble. Ten months after I went in, they took me outside to work with the mules—"

"Mules?"

Then on south, he thought, tracing lines on the brown paper, sneak across the Santa Fe tracks west of Albuquerque, keep on going south toward Quemado and Silver City, come out far west of El Paso and try the border there—

"Mules?" old Casper repeated.

"On the roads," Conant said. "With the scrapers. They put us skilled workmen out in the fresh air. Fourteen hours a day, old man, heaving a scraper behind a pair of jackasses. I worked at that till my parole come up and I put in. I was feeling friendly toward all the world. . . . I was turned down."

"But my God!" old Casper said. "You hadn't done nothin' real bad. Just a fight, the way I understand it."

"I hit the wrong man," Conant said. "The judge give

44

me ten but you know what that means in New Mexico. A year to fifteen months with good behavior. But I was turned down. It took me a while longer to wise up. I wasn't getting any parole, not for ten years."

"Glory be!" old Casper whispered. "I see what you mean now."

"Maybe you do," he said. "Maybe you don't. But I kept walking the chalk line, old man, because I was working outside those walls and I wasn't staying ten years."

"How long was it?"

"Two years and three days," he said. "I disremember the exact hours and minutes."

"But how," old Casper said, "how did you do it?"

Well, he thought, how had he done it? Even now he could not put that moment into words, the time that created itself unexpectedly at sunset, all of them working on the dusty road west of the prison, yanking the scrapers, driving the big mules, spitting cotton through the endless day. The spring rains had wet the earth and vanished, the adobe was brickhard again, so that roadwork became a cross no man could bear an entire summer. He had started the previous fall when it seemed easy, but the old cons told him no one could last a full summer. But he had to last, stay outside, if he got free. All through April he watched the guards on their horses, the two drivers who hauled them back and forth from prison on the wagons. He worked with fifty men, all trusties, men like himself from ranches and mining towns and little farms. There was a time when he gave up, and then he found the crack.

When they knocked off it was always on the verge of dusk; as they brought the scrapers to the sheds and turned the mules into the corrals, the mounted guards edged around to the water tank while the two big wagons lumbered up for their human cargo. There was a moment, if the afternoon was hot and dusty, when all the guards were around the corral at the water tank, leaving the two drivers and the head guard alone on the south side. Just a moment, no more than one minute before the first guard had watered his horse, himself, and trotted back into position.

No negligence was involved. These prisoners were all short-timers, doing no more than three years, and no one had caused trouble on the road crew in a decade . . . that much Conant learned from his cellmate. All else he saw and weighed and remembered.

The drivers had Winchesters, booted beside their seats. The mounted guards sheathed their rifles while watering the horses. It took a certain time—perhaps five seconds— to draw a rifle from its boot, aim, and fire. Then too, there was no strain of anger running constant between guards and prisoners, for no one was causing trouble or handing out cruelty. Conant had no special feeling toward the guards. He neither liked nor disliked them. They treated him fairly, especially the head guard who always stayed with the wagons and managed, each day at this time, to find a decent word for Conant. That was too bad . . . for the head guard. Conant was leaving this place, and no man could stand in his way.

When it happened, he moved in the instant, seeing and taking his chance. They put the mules in the corral and filed back on the road where the wagons were creaking up. The head guard was slouched in the saddle, rolling a smoke, talking with the rear driver . . . then it happened. One horse went on the prod at the water tank. Conant saw the horse buck high, saw the guard flounder in mid-air as he lost his stirrups. Dust rose and the other guards shouted gleefully as they closed in to calm the horse and lift the downed man. Conant was around the tailgate, coming up behind the head guard who stood in his stirrups and pointed out the fun to the driver.

Conant drew the iron bolt from inside his shirt—the twelve-inch bolt he had found three weeks ago and kept secreted in the mule shed daytimes—and ran forward in the shelter of the wagon. He leaped for the wheel, caught a spoke with his boot, climbed over the rim before the head guard turned. Conant struck him behind the ear, pushed him away and slugged the driver, flathanded into the saddle and caught the reins. He jerked the horse around and raced past the sheds toward the distant river. The other prisoners stood silent, giving him that precious time.

He was three hundred yards west before the lead driver saw him; and was so shocked he could not shout until Conant gained another hundred yards. He was six hundred in the clear, beyond rifleshot, before they collected themselves and started the pursuit.

And then, as Conant hoped, discipline slowed them. They had one iron rule of thumb: If a man escaped, watch the others, for the virus always spread. The second-in-command was forced to call off half his men to handle the other prisoners while he and four more spurred after Conant.

Conant jerked the Winchester from his saddle boot; it was fully loaded, one cartridge in the chamber, and he held it across his thighs as he broke downward into the cross-hatched network of ravines and arroyos, through the piñon and juniper that dotted the flats. The guards were unequally mounted, two drew far ahead and slowly closed the gap. Six or seven miles out, Conant dropped into a deep, twisting arroyo with one guard scarcely two hundred yards back, shooting now, coming dangerously close. Conant made a sharp bend, saw the rock slide ahead, and stopped the horse. He came off, holding the reins, and laid the Winchester over a rock. When the guard rounded the bend, fifty yards away, Conant shot him from the saddle. He levered the carbine and waited, hearing the other one seconds behind. When that guard ran into view Conant missed his first shot, levered frantically, and dropped him with the second.

He ran to them, pulling his horse, stripped holster and Colt from one, cartridges from both, smelling the blood and sweat, looking into the faces before he turned away. They were dead. He was up and riding instantly; when darkness came, he reached the river and turned north.

"Conant!" old Casper said.

"What?"

Old Casper was frightened. "What's the matter . . . did I say something wrong?"

"No," he said slowly. "Nothing, old man. . . . How did I do it? I grabbed a horse, cut for the river, shot two guards, and got clear. That's the size of it."

"Oh sure," old Casper said thinly. "And then you headed north?"

"Yes."

"East of the river?"

"At the start," he said.

He had thrown off the pursuit in darkness and gambled on the chance they might comb the west bank first. He rode through the night until he passed San Ildefonso and Santa Clara; on the edge of Espanola he found an empty farmhouse and exchanged his prison clothes for the shirt and trousers. He crossed the river and doubled back into the rising canyon trail, across the upper flats, and hid that

day in the trees behind the old Puye cliff dweller ruins on
the rim of the high cliff where he could see fifty miles
across the valley. That night he rode north past Ojo Caliente and camped in the forest; the next night he reached
Taos Junction and broke into the depot, hoping to find
telegraph message copies telling how the search was
planned. He found a copy notifying the local marshal,
but no more. He took the straw hat from the freight room
and headed eastward for the river. The horse dropped
dead ten miles from the river and he hid out through an
endless day in the timber covering those low hills and
ridges. That night he reached the gorge and descended
to the river, went upstream three miles from the bridge,
and passed the day in a juniper thicket. All that time he
had fled without thought. He made his way upriver until
he reached the mouth of Taos Creek gorge entering from
the east. He ascended that shallowing gorge, drawn instinctively to the mountains beyond Taos, thinking of
crossing the pass, returning to the country he loved. He
came to his senses at last, crouching in the willows below
the Casper farm.

"How come you headed this way?" old Casper asked.
"Eh?"

"They know where you worked," old Casper said.
"They were dead certain to guard the passes—Mora, Palo
Flechado, Red River. Didn't you figure that?"

"I know," he said.

"Changed your mind now?"

"It'll work out," he said.

"I know just what you're thinking," old Casper said
admiringly. "Is that man you hit still living over there?"

"Yes."

"At Springer, wasn't it?"

"Outside Springer," he said.

49

"And you want a crack at him," old Casper said. "By God, I would too. . . . Listen, how did it happen?"

"We come to town," he said. "In the saloon. Trouble started somehow, next thing he tried to pistol-whip me. We were all drunk; I took it away from him and worked him over. . . . I woke up in jail."

"Rich man?" old Casper asked.

"He'd fill the bill," Conant said. "He pressed charges the next month—"

"Next month!"

"When he come from the hospital," Conant said. "The judge give me ten."

"I don't blame you," old Casper said softly. "I'd feel the same way."

Conant looked down at the butcher paper where his pencil had drawn lines, traced a route over rivers and mountains and forests. He had no great desire to go east and find that man; for that way was death. He had no chance of working through fifty men into a ranch headquarters built like a prison. No, he wanted freedom, nothing more. Let the old man think what he wished, the way lay west and south, not east.

"I'd feel the same way," old Casper repeated. "You grow up in this country, Conant?"

Outside the sun was high, heating all the land, dissipating the coolness of the house.

"Rachel," he said curtly, "make a fresh pot of coffee."

"I am tied, señor."

"All right," he said. "Give me time."

Old Casper groaned and wiggled, easing his bones. He grinned at Conant and shook his head.

"I'd make a helluva lawyer, eh?"

"Why?"

"Asking you all this," old Casper said. "Here I start with the breakout and come back to why you were sent and then where you grew up. I got it all bass-ackward, eh?"

"Yes," Conant said. "We get things bass-ackward, old man."

Four

AT HOT MIDDAY OLD CASPER MASSAGED HIS BLUE-
veined hands and ate his plate of beans. Tony had listened
earlier, then slept as old Casper's voice droned on and on,
devouring the morning. Rachel cooked the meal, they
woke Tony and fed him; and now, his own hunger ap-
peased, old Casper watched Conant slyly. It was getting
him, Jesu yes, the way he answered questions with a thick
tongue and gulped black coffee.

"Son," he called.

"Yes, Father."

"You well?"

"Fine, thank you," Tony said politely. "And you?"

"Sore as a boil," old Casper grumbled.

"Go to sleep, Father."

"I'll try," old Casper said. "You talk with Conant. Be
nicer for him. I'm an old man and you two are the same
age."

"If he wishes," Tony said.

"Oh, go right ahead," Conant said sarcastically. "I'm

53

used to it now. William Jennings Bryan kept me looking for a ballot box all morning.''

Old Casper rolled over and faced the wall. He would not make his decision, set the time, until supper. He thought of the scene in town when they led the murderer into the plaza. Incongruously, a nursery rhyme of his childhood tinkled in his head. ''Rings on her fingers, bells on her toes!'' The bells turned golden and he was singing in his sleep.

Rachel scrubbed dishes in the cracked enamel pan, the yellow lye soap reddening her chapped hands. Conant stood in the doorway, face long and solemn with fatigue, the hard lines of cheek and jaw contorted like a *santo* condemned to eternal agony.

''Out of water?'' he asked.

''Yes,'' she said. ''But I saved a pot for coffee.''

''I'll get more tonight.''

No one had offered to carry water for three years in this house, or given consideration to her leg. Or spoken decent words to her. She lived with pain and neglect but he faced greater emptiness and trouble than she might ever know; and still he treated her with courtesy. Perhaps she puzzled him. She knew he was surprised at her calmness when he entered the house and the old man leaped up in a frenzy of fear; and then, when he saw how she lived, how they treated her, he became furious. Not at them; at her, for her meekness. After all, he had been a prisoner two years before he opened his door to freedom, and in all that time he had never lost hope. He would not accept that feeling of defeat in others, and he saw it in her. But she could not tell him how she waited, that her desire was no less than his. Her door, if she ever found it, did not lead outward. Her door would open her own house to her at last.

"You wish more coffee?" she asked.

"Put it on," he said gruffly. "You got a washtub?"

"No, señor."

"No tub, no nothing!" Conant said. "I need a bath."

"The creek, señor," she said mildly.

"Conant?" Tony called.

They were scheming now to capture him. She sensed it at breakfast when old Casper asked his innocent questions, sympathized with Conant, kept him awake. If the opportunity arose the old man expected her help as a matter of course, but her mind was firmly resolved. He was nothing to her, had never been, and she would not help. Old Casper had treated her like dirt too long, basked in his supposed superiority, but all the while she had merely suffered him. That was her secret triumph. He had called her useless a thousand times; now she would truly fill the role. Let him solve his own riddle.

"Conant?"

"Yes."

Conant moved to the bedroom door and her husband spoke for the first time that day. In his words Rachel saw the pattern. She knew that tone, that friendly man-to-man appeal. Tony would speak of horses and women and other trivial things. His talk skimmed the surface of life, just as his own life ran on, shallow and unthinking, engrossed only with himself. She could not escape those words . . . until nightfall when she chewed her peyote and closed her eyes.

"I think you worry for my black horse," Tony said.

"Why?"

"But he is in the pasture, eh?"

"Yes."

55

"I told you," Tony said. "He's a fine horse, he can run all day—"

"And night?"

"Perhaps," Tony said. "I have never punished him in that way."

"Forget it," Conant said. "You've got no sense of humor."

He glanced at Rachel, tested Tony's knots, and received a confidence-inviting smile.

"I worked once at Cimarron."

He gave the ropes a tug and returned to the door. The coffee was boiling, Rachel had moved to her cot. "Where?" he asked. He felt bad inside, the top of his head was light as white water froth.

"The Cross L's," Tony said. "You know it?"

"Yes."

"I broke horses," Tony said proudly. "They paid me three dollars, I made almost one hundred in a month."

"Run 'em on a spring rope?" he asked.

"Yes, in the corral," Tony said. "With the sack and one leg up . . . that is the best way, eh?"

"One way," Conant said absently.

He rubbed his hands and remembered the free years, horses under him, bucking against the boards and across the corrals of half-forgotten ranches, good and bad horses, meek and wild, tame and outlaw, but all free. Two years since he had smelled rope burns and felt a bronc between his legs.

"That was a fine job," Tony said. "And what a time I had at home."

"You married then?" he asked.

"Oh, no," Tony said. "That was seven—eight years ago. Did you know Taos then?"

"Some," he said.

56

"The best place in the world," Tony said happily. "Then and now. Everyone is your friend . . . and the women! Do you know our women, Conant?"

"No."

"It has been a long time for you, eh?"

"I don't need a pimp!"

Tony laughed merrily, refusing the insult. "I did not mean that, Conant, but if you wish when you leave us and ride west near Arroyo Hondo, go down the creek from the crossing to the fifth house on the north bank. Ask for Rosalia—"

"You know that house?" Conant said.

"Of course."

"A good house?"

"In excellent condition," Tony said. "You can tell by the yellow paint and the windows—three with real glass."

Conant looked at the fatuous fool on the bed. The fool who knew other houses more intimately than his own, who did not care if his own house fell down about his ears.

"How come you dug no well here?" he asked.

"The creek is so near," Tony said.

"That house in Arroyo Hondo," Conant said. "How far is it from the creek?"

"Oh, fifty, sixty feet."

"Got a well?"

"Oh yes, a fine well."

Conant said, "Where's your washtub, Rachel?"

"But you asked, señor," Rachel said. "I have none."

"How about a churn?"

"No, señor."

"What do you use?"

"I go to the neighbors."

Conant walked to the stove and jerked the iron holder

from the nail and slapped it over the sadiron. The catch was faulty, the claws slipped when he lifted.

"One sadiron," he said. "Got to reheat it all the time, eh?"

"Yes, señor."

"How come, Tony?" he called.

"I know nothing of those things," Tony answered. "That is woman's work. . . . Listen, I have been thinking of that prison—"

"And dishes," Conant said, glancing at the shelves. "Four plates, four cups, three knives, pot and kettle. Nothing decent for a woman to work with. Here . . . three spoons, three forks that maybe come out with Carson. Burned out stove grates, cracked lids, the stovepipe is rusty. One lousy lamp, no curtains on that window, and *no* glass. Dirt floor, no churn, no well . . . and you expect her to feed you, wash your clothes, do every little god-damned thing you want. Put her out here on a cot with a pair of second-hand issue blankets. And lay there telling me how to find women in good houses with glass in the windows. You miserable sonofabitch! You no-good—ah, what's the use."

"But, Conant," Tony said plaintively. "She's only a woman."

Conant glared at Rachel. What difference did it make? She had a choice. If she had any guts she'd walk out of here. She had a family somewhere in the valley, her parents would take her in, her brothers would defend her honor. Getting mad did him a world of good . . . not for her, but for him, It woke him, kept him thinking. That was the best idea: get so mad he forgot sleep. He laughed dryly.

"Conant?"

"My God," Conant said. "Don't you ever run down?"

"That prison . . . I have been thinking. I fell asleep this morning and did not hear how you escaped."

Conant swore in soft disgust. He could kick Tony in the privates, spit in his face, and it made no difference. Tony's kind refused insults when circumstances demanded such indifference. His kind waxed fat in the upper river valley. Strong, handsome, worthless to the bone. They lived for today and ignored tomorrow. They married and begat a flock of children, and scratched in foreign chicken yards before their firstborn was weaned.

"Conant, how did you do it?"

"Ask the old man," he said.

"But he's asleep."

"I don't repeat," Conant said thickly. "Figure it out yourself."

"Well," Tony said cheerfully, "I have been thinking of it and surely you were outside the walls, for I have never heard of one man escaping from within the prison. However . . ."

Conant moved to the cot in quiet desperation. He said, "Lay down, Rachel," and tied her. The voice continued, persistent as a buzzing fly. He wandered from door to window, back to the table, and sat heavily. The watch read two o'clock; four hours till supper, another three before he dared steal a little sleep. He flattened the butcher paper and studied the map he had drawn.

". . . is that not possible?" Tony was asking.

"Oh sure," Conant said. "Go on . . . keep talking."

Tony knew he had spoken foolishly, mentioning women, but his repertoire of conversation was limited. He slipped away from such dangerous subjects and spoke of the prison, but anger was boiling in him. Conant had insulted him grossly before his wife, made him appear mean and cheap and lazy. Wait, he thought, until tonight! He'd grind his heel in that face, lead the gringo into town like a bear on a chain. He talked on, obeying his father's command, and heard the heavy sound of Conant's breath.

"Rachel!" he said.

"Yes."

"Is he asleep?"

"He seems so."

Tony cursed in Spanish. "Wake him, you fool, wake him!"

"How?"

"Who cares?" Tony said furiously. "We must keep him awake, don't you understand? Do something!"

"I cannot move," she said.

"Scream," Tony said. "Make a noise."

"I am tired, my throat aches."

"Woman," Tony said ominously, "I'll remember this."

"You have no chance," she said.

"We have," he said. "Do you think that *cabrón* can outsmart my father and me? Oh no, woman. We'll get him."

"You cannot."

Tony cursed her indifference and yanked his ropes, twisted his body. He groaned and cried as if he galloped through horrendous nightmares.

"Oh," he shouted. "Ohhhh!"

A hand spun him, slapped his face. He stared blankly and threshed about while Conant continued to slap him.

"What . . . ?" he mumbled.

"Wake up," Conant said. "You sound worse dreaming."

"A terrible dream," Tony said sheepishly. "I was riding a pass—Red River, I think—and my horse slipped, oh, it was high up. I fell, I was caught in a tree, the tree was bending outward over the cliff—''

"My mistake," Conant said.

"Eh?"

"Woke you too soon," Conant said.

"Oh," Tony laughed. "You make the joke."

"Sure," Conant said bitterly. "But tell me all about it. I love to hear you talk."

"But I only—"

"Talk!" Conant said.

He left the bedroom and Tony moved his bruised face in triumph. He began talking of his dream, elaborated on the mythical dangers. The afternoon passed sluggishly, borne on the stubby wings of his cramped mind.

Staying awake was torture. Conant dared not sit long, and standing hurt his feet. He leaned against the wall and stripped off his socks; the blisters were raw, the stone bruises puffy, but no red lines crept upward, thank God, nor was the skin drum-tight. He smeared a fresh layer of salve on his feet, drew on the socks, and pushed timidly into the boots. He glanced at the map but the lines blurred, his eyes refused sharp focus. He stood in the doorway and watched the black horse graze in the pasture beside the creek; hummingbirds darted across the yard, a tough old rooster strutted from the chicken shed and cackled hoarsely. Conant ticked off the evening chores: feed the horse, carry water and wood, eat, take care of three people. Then, with luck, he could sleep a few hours.

"Ah, the dances, Conant!"

Tony was speaking of Taos dances, how the orchestra played all night. The thought made Conant sick, and the very idea of staying awake when a man could sleep. But the fool on the bed helped him. The voice nagged at his ears, kept him upright.

"The black horse," he said.

"Yes?"

"Where'd you get him?"

"From Fernando Castro at Questa," Tony said. "He is five years now, I got him at two."

"He's got some Kentucky in him," Conant said.

"Oh yes," Tony said. "He is from a Castro mare, the brown one, by Montoya's black stallion. . . . Montoya has the ranch at Amalia on the edge of the big Vermejo Park Ranch . . . you know it?"

"The man from Chicago," Conant said.

"Hah, you know of him," Tony laughed. "How he brought the thoroughbred studs to breed here. Montoya could not pay such fees but his mares roamed in the night. No stud fee then, eh? His black stallion came from that, and my black came from him. I paid forty dollars and broke him out myself . . . you see, for such a horse one hundred dollars is a fair price."

"Is he gunshy?"

"I have never hunted from him," Tony said. "I cannot say."

Conant heated coffee, untied Rachel, brought her a cup and glanced at the old man while she drank. Her leg pained badly, for her hands trembled on the yellowed china.

"More?"

"No, thank you, señor."

"Time to cook," Conant said. "But take it easy a while. We'll listen to the parrot."

"Parrot?"

"Hear him," Conant said. "In there on the bed. Man I worked for once had a parrot, got it in Juarez. Smart bird in one respect. Remembered everything it heard, reeled it right off. Only one thing wrong with parrots.''

''What is that, señor?''

''They never learn a word on their own,'' Conant said. ''Damn pretty feathers and no brain.''

Old Casper smelled food and opened his eyes. The wall was dark, the window had faded gray. He lay still, waking, sampling the room sounds: the stove, Rachel moving dishes, Conant shuffling his feet near the door, Tony's voice from the bedroom. Old Casper rolled over and groaned loudly.

''I don't like to complain but I ain't a young man no more. You got me tied so tight I can't feel nothin'.''

''What do you want?'' Conant said. ''A nice long walk?''

''Why sure,'' old Casper said. ''I won't go far.''

''Just to town, eh?''

''Hell,'' old Casper said. ''You think I'd stop there!''

''At least you got spunk,'' Conant said.

Old Casper saw Rachel fill a plate with beans and ham. He called, ''Son.''

''Yes, Father.''

''You sleep any?''

''A minute,'' Tony said. ''I had bad dreams and Conant woke me. We talked all afternoon.''

''Too bad I missed it,'' old Casper said. ''By God, I'm hungry!''

''In a minute,'' Conant said.

Old Casper cleared his mind and faced the night. It was time to decide. He watched Conant follow her into the bedroom, face heavy with exhaustion, feet barely clearing the floor. Yes, tonight was the time. Far past midnight

when Conant would sleep like the dead. Now he must do
everything perfectly or all was lost.

They came from the bedroom and Rachel knelt beside
him while Conant stood guard. She tugged at his knots,
the ropes loosened, his arms came free. Old Casper began
his role. He tried to sit up and failed. He grunted and
forced a thin hissing sigh between tight lips. Rachel pushed
him erect; he fell forward on his face.

"Work his arms," Conant said.

She revolved one arm, then the other, and old Casper
bellowed, face contorted, until one arm apparently lost the
sleep needles and came awake. He shook it weakly while
she exercised his other arm; it was fully ten minutes before
he sat upright, supporting himself on his flat hands.

"Just too old," he gasped. "Can't snap back any
more."

"Can you eat?" Conant asked.

"I'll try."

"Get his plate, Rachel."

Old Casper took the plate and handled the spoon with
clumsy fingers. He dropped his head against his chest and
fed like a baby in a highchair. He drank from his cup but
somehow the cup slipped and spilled on his pants. Conant
swore impatiently.

"Tie him up."

"Not yet," old Casper begged. "I won't even wiggle.
Give me a little time."

"Tie him up!"

Old Casper submitted to his ropes and lay groaning as
Rachel ate her meal, was tied, and Conant hunched over
his plate, eating, drinking scalding coffee, talking to himself.

"Now chores. . . ."

Old Casper watched him blunder outside with rifle and

bucket. His steps died on the creek path and Tony hissed, "Father?"

"Tonight," old Casper said.

"Good . . . he's in bad shape, Father."

"I know . . . remember what I told you?"

"Yes," Tony said eagerly, "but your arms—?"

"Hah," old Casper snorted. "Fooled you too. That's good. Now do it right."

"And then?"

"I'll tell you," old Casper said. "Leave it to me."

Conant filled the bucket, listened to the night, and swept off his straw hat. He dropped on the flat rock and thrust his head beneath the water. It struck ice cold and brought him up gasping, shivering. He ducked again and again, washed his face and neck, felt the icy water runnel down his back. When he turned with the bucket, the black horse trotted past him up the slope.

"In your turn," Conant said. "You'll get those oats."

He walked slowly to the house, emptied the bucket in the stove reservoir, made another trip and set the full bucket against the wall. "Plenty of wood," he said thankfully and crossed the yard to the shed. He pulled down hay and swore without anger as the black horse nudged him aside, impatient for the oats.

"I won't kill you," he said. "Not if you cooperate, horse."

He stepped outside and heard a hawk pass overhead, the shirring of wings as the hunter lifted from the creek to the hillslopes where mice scampered in the grass. He went on, back to the silent house, and touched off the lamp; light flared and pushed against the darkness.

"You first, Rachel," he said.

He led her unresisting and brought her back; and turned

to the old man. He loosed the leg ropes, untied the swollen hands, and boosted old Casper upright. The old man took one step and collapsed.

"Get up," he said.

"I'm trying," old Casper said weakly.

Three times the old man stood and fell. The third time he looked up hopelessly and shook his head.

"Better tie me. . . . I'll scrooch around, maybe I can make it."

"You want to go?" Conant snapped.

"Lord yes," old Casper said pitifully. "I got to go. . . . Take my son first. I'll make it in a couple minutes."

"All right," Conant said, "but I'm not wasting all night on you, old man."

He retied the ropes and took Tony into the night, marched him back and lashed him down. Then he untied old Casper and boosted him erect. Old Casper fell once, found his legs, and staggered from the house. At the corner he slumped against the wall and groaned.

"Give me a minute, eh!"

"Pretty bad?"

"I'm sorry," old Casper said humbly. "I know what's causing it."

"Muscles," Conant said. "I seen men come from solitary with the irons on. Same thing."

"No," old Casper said, slapping his arms across his chest. "It's the circulation. My arms tied behind, that cuts off the blood flow. I got them bad veins in my arm and back, you can see 'em. Another night and I'm scared one'll bust. I even have trouble talking—"

"Then you'll be dead," Conant said acidly.

"No, I'm plumb serious. . . . Listen, can't you tie my hands in front? Just tonight. I'm scared."

"No dice, old man."

"I won't try nothin'," old Casper pleaded. "Honest to God . . . what could I do anyway?"

"Get along," he said.

"Oh, forget it," old Casper said thinly. "What the hell's the use."

Conant marched him out and waited, and when they started for the house old Casper wobbled, banged against the door, fell beneath the window. Conant jerked his arms into the small of his back and old Casper cried in great pain.

"Please . . . please!"

"Oh, hell," Conant said. "You'd keep me awake all night."

He tied the old man's ankles and pulled both arms front, elbows against the round belly, and wrapped the rope three times about body and arms, pinning them together tightly. Old Casper could not lift hands to mouth lashed in this fashion. Conant double-knotted the wrists and wove the rope end into the lashings. Old Casper curled up tightly and mumbled vague thanks.

"Just don't die on me," Conant said.

He barred the door and turned down the lamp; and then he approached the chair that was prettier than any woman tonight. He laid the Winchester on the table and eased himself into the chair. The watch read five minutes of ten o'clock.

"Rachel," he said. "You all right?"

"Yes, señor."

"Tony?"

"Asleep soon," Tony said softly.

"Old man?"

Old Casper was asleep. Conant pulled the holster forward between his thighs and dropped his arms heavily on the table.

"No more talk tonight," he said. *"None.* One peep and I'll gag you with a sock."

Silence replied, soft-breathed and respectful. He drew the cup between his hands, sipped the cooling coffee, and then his head sank upon his forearms as blessed sleep loosened the bands that squeezed his brain.

Rachel saw him slump forward, move his legs beneath the table, unconsciously seek the most comfortable position. He snored resonantly as his body plummeted into unhearing sleep. The top of his head reflected lamplight, the stiff brown hair matted and unkempt, growing bushy above his protruding ears. There was no menace in him now; all men were innocent in sleep.

She lifted her bound hands and took the first peyote button. She chewed slowly, tasting the bitterness, waiting for peace and contentment, the dream that took her away. She chewed faster, seeing the old Ute's face, knowing he reproached her gently for hastening a natural spell; but he would forgive her if he understood. She chewed the second button and heard far off their voices murmuring, and then dreams claimed her. The ache in her leg was gone, she hated no one, and there were yet six buttons in her hand, with fifty more in the cubby behind the stove.

"Now?" Tony whispered.

"Wait."

"You've got it!"

Old Casper had it, a huge lump of lye soap burning his mouth. Returning to the house he'd almost gagged and spewed it forth, but falling, playing possum, diverted Conant's sight and smell. Now he rolled on his side and opened his mouth wide. He pushed the soap outward with his tongue, saw it drop beneath his nose. His throat contracted in a long-delayed paroxysm of coughing. He rammed his face into the floor and fought the involuntary contractions of his throat muscles.

"Father!"

"I've got it," old Casper said weakly. "Enough to choke a horse."

"And your hands?"

"In front."

"Can you do it, Father?"

"I'll do it."

"How long?"

"Hush," old Casper said. "Let me rest. I can't tell you. . . . Three, four hours."

He forced relaxation, breathing and exhaling deeply, evenly, until all his muscles were loose. He had worked through every step of this in his mind, what to try, how to change his plan if one way failed. He rested ten minutes by the count in his head, and then he began.

He lifted his legs, expelled his breath, and sucked in his round belly which had been expanded while Conant lashed his arms flat against his body. Now his arms moved beneath the ropes; he strained them upward in their shoulder sockets, pressing both elbows into his sides. An inch, two inches . . . the knots on his wrists caught in the lashings, he was forced to inhale. But he had expected this: He must continue to expand his belly, stretch those ropes, then draw inward and lift his arms; and he must work slowly, without sound, even though Conant was deep in sleep. Old Casper had estimated two hours to free his arms; as he pulled, time and again, and his wrists caught, it seemed he could not succeed. He worked on in the silence, lamplight flickering, throwing curious shadows, his son lying on the bed in breathless hope. It seemed hours before the unending push-suck brought the lower lashing an inch nearer his hips and, the wrist knots cleared, his

69

hands came through. Two ropes to go, he thought, and he must work faster.

The second rope was cleared in minutes but the last was twisted into his shirt and refused to come down. Old Casper turned and watched Conant narrowly; satisfied, he lay flat on his back and pushed himself against the floor with his heels. He progressed snail-like in a circle; the floor rasped against his shirt, caught the rope, forced it downward. It gave an inch, another, and loosened. Old Casper expelled his breath in one great effort; his shoulders rose, his elbows pressed into his sides cruelly; his wrist knots caught, slipped, and broke free.

Old Casper raised his arms, pressed his bound hands against his mouth, and kissed them.

And now! He hunched around and located the soap with his fingertips. His mouth made contact, his teeth bit off a small piece; and then he began the worst part.

Using his mouth as a tool, old Casper laboriously soaped the rope that wound around and between his wrists. His head bobbed like a woodpecker as he probed into the crannies between the knots, rubbing soap against the rope; and that was only the beginning. Once he had soaped the knots and exposed rope, he must pick those knots with his teeth, loosen them, spread the soap further.

Old Casper raced time, his body growing hot and wet with sweat. Time and again he rested his aching jaws, spat to clear his throat, tore off small chunks of soap and rubbed them on the ropes. Conant had cinched the knots so tightly that each, a rough knob, seemed impervious. Old Casper reached a state of near-panic. The soap was gone, his jaw was numb, his gums were bleeding; then the first knot gave beneath his teeth; he pulled as his head strained backward.

"Ahh!" he said.

"Father?"

"Quiet," old Casper murmured.

He rested a moment and attacked his wrists with furious bites and yanks; and slowly the knots fattened and limbered. Old Casper raised his hands high, pushed his nose between the dirty palms, found the last knot. He caught the key strand in his teeth, worried and pulled, and the rope came free. Before his staring eyes, his hands separated and flexed.

Old Casper reached down between his knees and grasped the knots circling his ankles. He scraped soap from the wrist ropes and worked it into those knots; and long after, nearing exhaustion, his legs fell apart. He turned slowly and glanced at Conant, sprawled on the table. It took great restraint to lie still, exercise his arms and legs, wait for feeling to surge through his body. When he was certain, old Casper came up on flat hands, straightened, stared at the rifle ten short steps away. He saw himself go forward, take up the rifle . . . but he could not do it alone.

Nor had he planned it that way. On hands and knees, he crawled slowly into the bedroom and leaned against the bed.

"Quick," Tony said. "Quick, Father."

"Patience," old Casper whispered.

He leaned across the bed and found the knots; in short minutes Tony swung his feet to the floor, bent down beside old Casper who spoke in the nearest ear.

"Listen now . . . the two-by-four in the corner. I'll take that. Follow me into the room. Go to the left, me to the right. Not a sound, you hear, not a sound! When we reach the table, watch me. I'll raise the club and say, 'Go!' Then I'll hit him on the head and you get the rifle . . . understand?"

"Yes," Tony said thickly. "Look at him sleep, Father. Look at him. . . . Oh, we owe him the big debt!"

"Hurry now," old Casper said. "It's almost light."

While he labored, night had passed into the pre-dawn grayness. Old Casper felt in the corner beside the door, found the three-foot length of wood used as a doorstop, and hefted it in his right hand.

"Now," he said.

He advanced and his son followed. He moved to the right, his son angled to the left. Conant slept on, head in arms, body stretched slackly between chair and table, supported by head and hips. Old Casper glanced at Rachel, saw her staring wide-eyed at the ceiling, unseeing, uncaring. He tiptoed toward the end of failure and frustration, holding the club like a cross of gold. He was a dedicated man in that moment. With nothing to lose, he staked all. He reached the table and lifted the club above his head. His son was poised, hands clawed, ready to leap and take up the rifle. Old Casper looked across the table at that tousled head and tensed all his muscles.

"Go!" he cried.

Five

WHEN A MAN SLEPT IN A CHAIR FACING A TABLE, HEAD pillowed on folded arms, his legs were invariably thrust beneath the table, shaping his body like a jackknife with blade one-quarter open. His back was concave, his stomach bobbed gently upon his thighs to the regular movement of his lungs. Two results were inevitable: His unconscious shifting nudged the chair backward, his head slowly approached the table edge. If he slept long enough the time came when his head, hanging on by a whisper, dropped away. Nothing serious happened. His head fell, his arms flailed, he struggled instinctively to regain his balance. A sleep-drugged man could slip, recover, and resume his position without waking.

At four o'clock in the morning Conant had reached that precarious state. His body weight pushed the chair one last inch, his forearms and head dropped below the table-top level. All this occurred in one fraction of a second; one moment in his life, too small for measure, unimportant under ordinary circumstances. But falling in the same split second, Conant heard a shout and was shocked brutally awake by violent pain in his left shoulder. Old Casper's club struck the exact spot his head had filled one moment earlier; it splintered on the table edge and the muscled cushion of his shoulder.

Conant cried out in pain, and pain woke him as he sprawled on his right side. He looked upward and saw old Casper's face registering triumph, then disbelief, then horror, all in the moment of Conant's fall; and there was Tony lunging across the table, hands snatching at the rifle. Old Casper roared in terror and swung his club again; but a strange thing happened as Conant fell.

The club blow jarred the table and Conant's left arm gave the edge a forward shove. Tony's fingers overshot the mark; instead of grasping breech and barrel, they struck the bare wood half an inch beyond the rifle. Conant saw all—club, faces, fingers, eyes—as the lamp tipped slowly from the table and crashed to the floor, showering his cheek with flying splinters of glass. In that moment he responded instinctively, an animal fighting for life. He rolled beneath the table, escaping the second swipe of old Casper's club, and his body accomplished two desperate acts of rebuttal: He clawed at his Colt tangled in his crotch and reared upward under the table with a violence that surpassed theirs.

"Hit him!" Tony shrieked.

"Get the rifle!" old Casper bellowed.

But the lamp had smashed, the light was out, the abrupt darkness blinded them momentarily. Conant upset the table in their faces and sent the Winchester clattering away. Tony was spun into the stove and old Casper, lifting his club a third time, tried to chase Conant under the table, only to meet the rising top and sail backward, thrown off his feet.

"Tony!" old Casper cried.

Conant finally got his Colt free and scrambled to his feet. Instinct again warned him that old Casper was the most dangerous. He dived across the table and hit the old man in the act of scuttling toward the door. Old Casper howled as Conant shoved the Colt into his back.

"Tony!" he cried again.

Conant had the hammer half-thumbed before he stopped; he dared not risk a shot. He lowered the hammer and sapped old Casper on the right arm. The club dropped and the old man rolled over, pummeling Conant with his left. Conant smashed down twice before he connected with old Casper's head and choked off his yells.

"Father!" Tony called from the stove.

Conant turned and rushed, and his foot tripped over the lost rifle. He went sailing and his shoulder rammed Tony. Tony bounced away and rolled invisibly across the floor, gained his feet and ran for the door.

"Hold up!" Conant said.

The bar was raised and cast aside, the door came open. Conant ran, his foot hit the table, and he fell outstretched, crying with the pain in his swollen foot. Not six inches away old Casper wailed feebly,

"Son . . . son, help me!"

Conant paused to hit old Casper on the head and flatten him without a groan; then he followed Tony from the house into the cold darkness that preluded dawn. He ran halfway to the shed and stopped; feet thudded on the path, kicking pebbles, taking great jumps down the slope into the pasture. Tony was running for his life, taking huge strides on the familiar path. Conant followed, his socked feet striking sharp rocks and gravel, his left arm still stiff at his side. He left the path and veered across the wet grass to cut off Tony's flight toward town, but Tony knew these bottoms and ran like a deer. And then Conant heard him fall, splash full length in a cowhole, not far below in the deep shadow of the willows.

"Hold it," Conant called softly. "Hold it, Tony!"

Tony was frightened unto death but he could not see Conant; therefore, one part of his mind reasoned clearly. What Conant could not see, he could not shoot. But their paths were converging and Conant, having made up lost ground while Tony rose from the water, had drawn ahead and was certain to block off the creek trail.

"Hold it," Conant said again.

Tony turned off the trail and plunged into the willows. Conant heard him crash inward toward the creek; and now faint grayness tinged the sky and the willows loomed black before him; water shone in the distant creek. Conant slipped into the mat of branches and slender stalks, feeling his way, slipping and pushing until he reached the bank; there he stopped. Tony Casper, downstream no more than thirty steps, had anticipated him and paused. Conant had no time for parlor games. The old man might recover and get away. How much time he had did not matter; seconds or minutes, all depended on the thinness of old Casper's skull and the rising panic in the man so near. Conant spoke softly in the night.

"All right, Tony. Now I'll kill you!"

He moved downstream ten stick-slapping, mud-sucking steps, and stopped abruptly. But Tony had not moved. Conant took three steps and paused in mid-stride; if Tony tried to match him step for step, he could not always freeze in perfect time. Conant took one step and paused; and heard the rustle.

He ran along the bank, branches slapping his face and arms; and stopped once more. Tony bolted from the nearby darkness and crashed through the last fringe of willows, floundered in the soft mud at the water's edge, plunged outward with a loud splash. Conant turned and waded into the creek, fifty feet wide here above the beaver dam, cold black water reflecting faint prisms of starlight on the ripples.

"You might as well stop," he said.

Not ten steps below, Tony plunged and waded toward the north bank where the cliff rose a hundred feet, offering sure escape if he could reach the rabbit warren of rock and tree and brush that lay between creek and cliff. Conant breasted the icy water, holding the Colt high, going waist-deep, then to his chest. Tony pushed and swam, and Conant matched him, knowing that Tony was either frightened beyond fear or cunning enough to guess that Conant would shoot only as a lost resort . . . and perhaps not then.

Conant's left arm moved finally to his command and he drew ahead as they neared the north bank. He gained three strides and suddenly went down in the deep pool beneath the rocky cliff. He swam, caught bottom with his toes, climbed until his head broke clear, and gambled all. He dove downstream with the current and caught Tony struggling upward through the mud into the overhanging willows. He lost the Colt as he grappled, and his left hand was weak in the fingers. He closed with a bigger, stronger man, knowing he must end it quickly before his strength drained away.

He took blows on his face, went for Tony's throat, and got his hold. He lunged backward into deep water, sucked air, and pulled Tony beneath the surface. Tony's hands found his throat as they bumped along; now it was life against life. Conant would not loosen his grip if they both ended in the jumble of sticks and brush at the foot of the beaver dam. He worked his legs around Tony's middle as the stars began to shine; the lights burst and wavered, spots danced before his open eyes. . . . It had come to this: who would give up? With the thought, Conant felt surrender. Tony's hands dropped, he struggled toward the surface and life-giving air. Conant rose with him in waist-deep water and dragged him toward the south bank by the neck.

The crossing was a nightmare. He pulled and slapped until they staggered blindly through the willows and up the path. Conant was in a frenzy. He ran Tony across the yard into the house; and there, moving in a drunken circle, old Casper crawled on hands and knees, head wobbling like a blinded bull. Conant kicked the old man on his back and threw Tony down at his side. Gray dawnlight dissolved the darkness as he found the ropes and tied old Casper sketchily. When he pulled Tony toward the bedroom he stopped in four rubbery steps and shook his head. The bed was an insurmountable height. He blundered to the bed, found those ropes, and tied Tony where he lay against the wall. Then he crossed to the overturned table and stared at the shattered lamp.

"No fire?" he said. "I'll be damned!"

He heaved and tugged, the table rose and thumped upright. He found the Winchester and held it tenderly, standing in the spreading puddle of oil and glass. He wanted rest but there was no choice: He must finish the work before full light.

"Worse'n herding sheep," he said idiotically.

He crossed the yard to the shed where the black horse stamped in hungry impatience. He pulled down hay, poured oats, rested briefly while the horse ate. Returning to the house he untied Rachel and took her into the morning and brought her back, retied her hastily, and stood in the doorway.

"Shot in the pants with luck," he said thickly.

No one moved in the creek bottoms. The sun burst orange-red above the valley and flooded past him, casting a slanting bolt on old Casper's body.

"I'll get to you," he said.

He lit the fire and made coffee, put on a kettle of water while he unbuckled his holster belt and cast it aside. He laid the Winchester on the table, gathered up the scattered rifle cartridges from the floor, and placed the little .32 banker's special beside them. They were all watching him now: the old man, beaten and bloody, Tony in his sopping clothes, the girl on her cot. There were as many degrees of feeling in them as hearts in their bodies. No one felt the same about anything. Paradise to one was poison to another. They watched him undress and stand naked, drinking coffee, and they waited for the explosion.

Conant was silent. He dried his body that contrasted unhealthy white against his sunburned face and hands, washed his feet, smeared on fresh salve and dry socks. He brought clothing from the bedroom and dressed in Tony's too-large shirt and trousers. He dropped the .32 into a hip pocket and took up the Winchester. Old Caper's eyes were fear-wide in his misshapen face. Conant moved to the doorway and spoke in a dull, soft voice as if he did not care how his words sounded or what they meant; but storms began the same way with vagrant gusts of soft wind and a harmless haze across the sky.

"I used to be quite a talker," he said. "But Santa Fe wrung me out and hung me up. There was no reason to talk, everybody had the same ideas. I feel better today. Maybe getting wet oiled the rusty joints. I feel like making a real come-to-Jesus speech, one of those barn-burners, the kind you hear at a camp meeting where the preacher has 'em sprouting wings and mounting the tent pole. In case you're wondering about that, I'm not talking through my hat. My old man was a preacher. You'd never guess it by my manners and such. Oh, he was no certificate preacher. He heard a call, the way my mother told it, when I was six months old. That was in north Texas. He dropped everything, sold a good farm, bundled us into the wagon with the furniture and stove, and headed west where the sinners were thick. Three days out he remembered what he forgot—the good book—but by then I guess he was writing his own. I don't recall him plainly. He left Raton when I was seven or eight. By then the call had left him and he headed north. I was older when my mother told me he took another woman with him. Seems like he heard a different kind of call. I don't know if he saved her. He'd never save himself.

"That was a fine sleep, almost six hours to my reckoning. I could use sixty but I'll take six and thanks. It was kind not to have those nightmares and wake me up, but I'm afraid you didn't get much sleep. I felt the soap and your teethmarks, old man. You ought to take better care of your grinders at your age. . . ." His voice moved on evenly against the brightening day, his face was composed as he turned from the doorway and nudged old Casper's wrists with one toe. "That was a good trick. I never figured on it. The soap was out back, I know that, but you didn't bring it inside in your hands because that's good old lye soap and I'd smell it easy. So you had it in your mouth . . . remember how we got our mouth washed out when we were kids? And you never spoke a word while I fell asleep. Then you scrooched around and got loose, untied Tony, and that club was in the bedroom all the time. I missed that—" he laughed softly and rubbed his left shoulder— "yes Lord, but I can feel it now. You like to busted my bones, old man, but you sure woke me up fast. I got to admire the way you charged me but you never learned one lesson: When you start something, play it straight through to the end. Otherwise you get nothing. Oh, you still had a chance when the lamp went over. I don't know as I could handle you both in the dark with the rifle and club skittering around loose. . . . If you wonder what happened outside, old man, don't be ashamed of Tony. He done his level best and it come down to me being a better duck or having bigger lungs . . . and you not having a hard head, although I admit you fooled me there. I estimated about six inches of bone between your ears. Still, it was close, too close, and I never want to try it again."

Conant began walking back and forth from the bedroom to the front door, his voice deepening as he talked.

"Understand, I don't blame Tony. He's just a sheep trailing the bell goat. Now I've got to tie you real tight, both of you, and these ropes are too puny for men of your caliber. I saw a skin in the shed—cow, I guess—and tonight I'll cut some thongs and we'll do the Comanche trick with you hombres." He grinned down at old Casper and spoke slowly in Spanish. "Do you understand, old gentleman, you with the filthy tongue? . . . No, don't talk, old man. I'll do the talking. I can read and write, too, and I speak Spanish very well. I heard what you called me that first day. I talk it better than you or Tony or even Rachel. I even know dialects. I grew up on a place where my mother cooked when we left Raton, and the only English I heard for seven years was the printing on the canned goods. Yes, I learned it young and I got my college degree as far south as Durango and west to the Gulf. I wish to God I'd stayed in Sonora . . . yes, that's where I'm going, old man. Back to Sonora. I won't lie to you. There's no need for it now. I don't think you'll try again. We'll see . . .''

He turned in midstride and pushed the Winchester muzzle against old Casper's dirty neck.

"You never should have tried it. Now I've got no confidence in you. Nobody was hurt, you were fed and watered, but you saw that thousand dollars shining in your eyes . . . come for me with a club, beat my brains out, haul me into town like a coyote and collect your bounty."

He walked away to the table, placed the Winchester carefully at his elbow, and rolled a cigarette.

"Yes, I admire anybody who stands up to trouble. Tony was better than you in some ways. He fought me right down to a frazzle, so maybe I misjudged him. . . . Well, you lose a thousand dollars but it's not much—" Conant smiled and his voice was coldly soft. "You think of all kinds of things on a morning like this. Mostly they don't amount to a hill of beans but I guess none of us has got the proper equipment for deep thinking or sermonizing. Sometimes the call gets into me but so far the loudest yells sound like drinking, women, and bicycle playing cards . . . and shooting straight. I've been thinking how lucky I am, and how damned foolish some folks can be. I'm lucky to be alive. You're damned lucky too . . . lucky to stay alive."

For the moment he was run down, like a dollar watch chasing midnight. He had told them exactly what he thought and how he felt, but in doing so he yanked up the shade guarding his private life and gave them a look inside. It made him think of life's endless surge, all the people coming in their countless multitudes with all their hopes, beliefs, desires, plans, talents—none of which could be preserved beyond a moment in time. Old Casper had convinced himself that he understood Conant and acted accordingly, but old Casper had been wrong, as his present position proved. He missed the point. Just as no man could stop living, he could not stop changing. A man changed from day to day. The deacon one day could be the devil's pitchfork the next. Just when you achieved— somewhat in the manner of a revelation—a thorough understanding of yourself or someone else, life ripped another day, month, year off the calendar, and outgrew all your hard-earned knowledge. You fell back to begin again but the truth was, as old Casper had learned so painfully, you never really caught up, not even with your own muddled state of affairs. Old Casper had misjudged his capacity to absorb pain and fight against death because, long before they met, Conant had settled his account with death. The hard, desperate part of facing an ending had come long ago, in prison. As time went on all the foolish, stupid dreams had atrophied and their dried remnants held a preliminary funeral. Now he had nothing to lose and all his life to gain.

"Rachel," he said. "You're not sleeping."

"No, señor."

"Hungry?"

"Yes."

"Why didn't you say so?" Conant growled. "You've got a tongue."

He untied her and sat at the table while she filled the coffeepot and sliced ham into the pan.

"For all?" she asked.

"They put in a full night's work," Conant said. "We'll fatten 'em up."

Rachel had awakened when they approached Conant. She saw the quirk of fate that upset the lamp and changed them from triumphant heroes into cowards fleeing death. Even before the chair slipped she had felt, somehow, that Conant would not be taken. By them, at least, for she knew them too well. The old Ute had spoken many times of those unfortunate men whose best efforts continually met with disaster. Old Casper was a prime example. He had chased success many times and, each time he had gained a summit and reached forward for the final goal, he stubbed his toe and fell. Tony had even less to recommend his possible success. He had never attempted such a height in their year of courtship and three years of marriage. She had watched them both try and fail, and her indifference to their fate was ground and rooted into her own total indifference. They had hurt her so badly she felt nothing for them, she cared nothing for herself. People were always hurt the worst by love; it had hurt her beyond pain, nothing else could be half as bad. Old Casper and Tony were afraid of death but thanks to them she was not afraid to die. She had died a little every day for three years and from that came courage, the only true kind—an understanding of danger that made her immune to any threat of death.

But their failure had pointed out a new hope for her, and Conant encouraged that faint spark when he asked if she had a tongue. From his rough consideration, unthinkingly offered, he had suddenly opened her eyes and stopped her from sliding along the same level with those two. Not that she counted for much or amounted to anything worth saying prayers or lighting candles for, but even in the worst times she had kept an awareness of life and the land about her, all the movement of nature and the feeling of people. For three years she had salvaged nothing but the living pattern of earth and air, flowers and birds, dashes of color and bursts of song; beyond those free gifts which no one could destroy, she had nothing. And now, her thoughts clarified by two successive nights of peyote dream and vision, she wanted to stay and grapple with old Casper and her husband on her own terms for the first time. And strangest of all, forming in her mind as she watched them fail, was an idea. They had failed and, in failure, showed her the way . . . if she wanted to try.

"Better turn those eggs," Conant said.

"Yes, señor."

"Take the old man first."

She served old Casper while Conant stood beside her with the rifle. Old Casper was in bad shape. The Colt barrel had lacerated his scalp and raised a pair of ugly lumps. He ate moodily, his eyes on his plate, trying to assemble his ruined dreams. Oh, she knew him so well, this dirty old man who treated her like a barn door. He would attempt no more violence, but now his thoughts were turning to the fine arts of wheedling and beseeching. Soon his whines would fill the house.

But moving to her husband, helping him sit up, she felt a subtle change alien to the man she knew. Tony was wet and battered, all his high color and foolish energy and handsomeness vanished, leaving him bereft of visible assets. And yet, when he handed up his empty plate, his eyes flickered with deep emotion. Somehow, somewhere, Tony Casper had acquired sufficient depth to feel true anger. Against her or Conant, she could not tell, but he had not surrendered.

"Wash your dishes," Conant said.

She turned to the stove and heated water while Conant tied Tony and resumed his seat. She chipped soap into the dishpan and scrubbed the greasy plates. Today and tonight and tomorrow, she thought absently, what would they bring?

"What are you doing?" Conant asked sharply.

She discovered herself behind the stove, taking down herbs from the cubbyholes, her fingers opening the tobacco sacks and removing pinches of sage and thyme and mint, but concerned altogether with the peyote buttons in her secret hiding place.

"For tonight," she said meekly. "Herbs for the beans."

"All right," Conant said quietly. "Go ahead."

Rachel placed her cutting board where Conant could see it plainly; but her arm, reaching into the cubbyholes, was hidden from his view. She did not really know why she did so, but as she chopped the herbs she brought down peyote buttons and sliced them thinly, ground them into powder and returned that fresh powder to the hiding place. She worked steadily through the morning until she had sliced and crumbled the peyote into fine powder; and then it seemed she understood her reason. The old Ute had warned her many times that should a person seek deeper dreams and visions, it was necessary to take a greater amount of peyote in a shorter period of time. It was impossible to eat such a large number of buttons, but if one made a powder and steeped it in a cup of tea, strange and miraculous results were sometimes achieved. Perhaps that was what she wished tonight.

Old Casper sat against the wall beside the south window, time passing like a familiar land seen through a slow train window. He reviewed every moment of the night and found no fault with his plan. He had conceived it brilliantly, carried it through to the climax without a hitch, yet here he sat with a sore head and no hope for the future. He disregarded the fact that he had quailed when they missed at the table. All he knew was that Conant had turned into a devil. He had been afraid then, but that fear was childish compared to the feeling Conant generated as he talked.

If he had ranted and raved, kicked their ribs in, old Casper would have understood. But that soft coldness, the words running on, probing into personal secrets that spread like tree roots into the innermost secrets of old Casper himself, all that had frozen the very blood in his veins. Old Casper forgot the thousand dollars. All he wanted now was his life. He did not care if he lay bound, hungry, and thirsty for a week before someone came. He could survive those petty indignities. But now he could not be sure that Conant intended to leave him alive. Conant had become a different man. Old Casper gathered his scattered assets and prepared for the afternoon and night. All his hole cards were gone. He had to make a winning hand from deuces.

He watched Conant clean the little .32, empty the wet cartridge belt, separate the Colt cartridges from the rifle and toss them aside.

"Yes," Conant said suddenly. "I lost the Colt."

Old Casper groaned to cover his surprise; it had not appeared Conant was conscious of his watching.

"What's the matter?" Conant said. "Your head giving trouble?"

"Nossir," old Casper said, with his first feeble attempt at jocularity. "But you sure walloped me a good one."

"Twice," Conant said. "The last one took, eh?"

"I never knew what hit me," old Casper agreed.

"Well, I was that close too," Conant said. "You might have split my skull with that two-by-four."

"No," old Casper said, "Wood ain't that hard—"

"Neither is my head," Conant said. "You better get some sleep. This afternoon you can lubricate that long tongue again and tell me some fairy tales. You'll like that, won't you."

"Yessir," old Casper said meekly.

"The way I estimate you," Conant said, "you just scratched the surface. I'll be looking forward to a real enlightening afternoon and evening."

Old Casper rolled over and dropped his battered head on the floor. His mouth tasted metallic with a fear he did not understand.

"Wish I had a drink," he mumbled.

"What brand, old man?"

"Gin," old Casper said.

"Your favorite, old man?"

"Yessir," old Casper said, overjoyed to find a subject that did not bring that subtle cruelty in Conant's retorts.

"Why? . . . you like the juniper?"

"You bet," old Casper said.

"Well, that proves it," Conant said softly. "You love that juniper taste in the gin . . . but why buy it with a million juniper berries around here? Just strip off a handful and sniff 'em up. Old man, you always run true to form. Yes, that's you in a nutshell. Or most everybody for that matter. People want to buy everything when most of their needs are right in the backyard. Yes, it comes down to that."

"Yessir," old Casper said forlornly.

Six

AFTERNOON WORE ON, HOT AND SILENT, SPASMODIC wind puffs stirring the dust. The black horse loafed in the willow shade beside the creek, the scraggly yellow chickens pecked in the sunbaked yard, all the birds had folded into the shadow of trees and cliff. Old Casper and Tony slept through morning into afternoon, insensate as grubs in the earth.

"What is the hour, señor?" Rachel asked.

"Three," Conant said. "The way you been working, that ought to be good *paella.*"

"You know it?"

"Sure," he said, "but no chicken."

She spread her hands helplessly. "They are outside."

"Can't be helped."

"But I had the rice, and I cut the ham very small."

"Better start it," Conant said. "Got enough wood?"

"I think so."

"Say, you put in chili?"

"Only a tiny pinch for you, señor."

"Spoon it in," Conant said. "What's the matter, you think I don't like chili?"

"I did not know—"

"Why, I was damn near weaned on it," Conant said. "Nothing like chili to keep you awake."

"Ah," she said, glancing at the cold pot. "You wish more coffee, señor?"

"Not now," he said. "I don't need it."

But he lied. He had slept six wonderful hours, then the fight sapped all that new-stored strength and left him weaker than before. He faced the grim reality of night and coming day . . . and refused to consider tomorrow night, riding westward for the river. His chance of escape had become a huge worry occupying all his thoughts, a worry reduced to its final and absolute form: what to do with three people!

They presented a problem in simple division. Three people were the divisor; a certain number of hours, those reckoned from the minute he left the house until someone entered, was the dividend; and the quotient, the end result, was his chance of living. Simple and unworkable, there was no way of coming at a true answer. Nobody could put down numbers and find life. But if the divisor was changed from a living number to a dead . . . "No," he said softly, but there was no finality in his voice.

"You are ill, señor?"

"Talking to myself," Conant said. "Which reminds me, we've got our own show here, free of charge. Old man, wake up!"

Old Casper grumbled in his troubled sleep and curled tighter against the wall. Conant pushed him over and shook him awake.

"Tony," he said. "Wake up!"

"I am awake," Tony said coldly.

"Stay that way," Conant said. "You might miss something important. Here we've got the second Eddie Foy himself and half the day wasted pounding our ear. . . . Old man, I'd give you that drink if I had it."

"Eh?" old Casper said thickly. "God . . . my head!"

"Time for the tent show," Conant said, "Remember?"

"Oh," old Casper said, working himself upright. "Anything you say, Conant. I'll try."

"That's the spirit," Conant said admiringly. "You sort of embarrass me, old man. All I got to do is name the tune and you stand ready to deliver. Why, I'd bet my shirt if I had one of my own, that you can talk on anything from A to Z and not miss a lick in between. Like that burro that had so much fodder he starved making up his mind which stack to eat. That's me—but I don't know if I want to hear about your fight with the Comanches or getting drunk with Allison or shooting up Lincoln County with the Kid. They don't appeal much to me, the way I'm situated, so maybe we ought to . . . say, you know poetry?"

"Sure," old Casper said.

"I was afraid you did," Conant said unhappily. "I don't like poems. Maybe we ought to have a debate. Now what could we wrangle over, gnaw at and kick around? Understand, I can't have you stacking the deck on me. Being an ignoramus, I want a fair shake. We could argue religion but that always causes bad feeling. We could argue politics but we both know how things go here. You'd vote more headstones and end up governor. Me, I'd be dogcatcher with luck. No, that won't do. We've got to come closer home and here I am in your house, eating your food, wearing your clothes and wearing out my welcome to boot. That's a good subject for debate—the state of your house, old man. You own this place free and clear?"

Old Casper rustled uncomfortably. He was conscious of a corner closing upon him in some mysterious way.

"Yes," he said hesitantly.

"How many acres?"

"Three hundred," old Casper said, "but I can't see any debate in that."

"Three hundred left from what?"

"Around a thousand," old Casper said.

"But you sold off seven hundred, eh?"

"I had to," old Casper said. "A man's got to eat and feed his family."

"And drink," Conant said. "And roust around. You damn sure put nothing into improvements. But you raised up your son, didn't you?"

Old Casper's position, bad as it was, could not entirely destroy his pride. "I sure did, and all by myself."

"I'll bet he was a good boy," Conant said. "Tony, were you a real good boy?"

"I do not know," Tony said stiffly.

"You don't *know?*" Conant said. "Why, Lord above. I knew what I was. Just about the meanest boy that ever grew up. I swiped pies off the pantry window and tied knots in the lariat ropes and put burrs under the saddle blankets and—why, there was no end to what I did, the trouble I caused. . . ."

All through the dying afternoon Rachel listened to him tease and bait them. He slumped in the chair, eyes heavy, and only his voice betrayed his watchfulness. He prodded old Casper into reluctant recollection of years and deeds hopefully forgotten; he thrust sharp daggers of memory deep into Tony. He was consciously cruel as he turned those shoddy years inside out. But why, she thought, why did he speak so? To stay awake, to pass time, to dominate them for once and all? Surely not to stay awake, for he could drink coffee and walk the floor, let old Casper pander to him, pass the slow hours that lay heavy on them all. And not to dominate them. He had finished with that foolishness from them. Old Casper was trying to read his mind and discover what lay in store for them, but thought of escape was over.

As afternoon lengthened and the *paella* filled the room with rich smell, she sensed the continued uncertainty in Conant, the reaching toward a decision he could not make. At six o'clock he sniffed the pot and called for supper; and once fed he took them into the night, each in turn, and brought them back. He carried water and wood, fed the horse, brought the cowhide from the shed and cut it into thin strips. He bound old Casper and Tony in a fashion strange to her. But one thing she saw: They would not escape from the rawhide lashings.

"You don't savvy this?" Conant asked.

"No, señor," she said.

"No matter," he said, "but I'll play teacher and spell out the ABC's for you. Tony stays out here because it gets lonesome and I want everybody to keep me company. The old man's under the window, Tony at the bedroom door. Looks dangerous, having them so close together, but the old man is tied to the window frame and Tony's cinched to that door post. About four foot of slack each, tied in a loop around their necks and back where they can't get to it. There's room to sleep but a man better not start pitching, get those nightmares. Because once he loses the slack that hondo tightens up and won't turn loose. It just gets tighter. A man can throttle himself easy. And I just might not wake up and help him out. True, old man?"

"Yessir," old Casper said meekly.

"Well now," Conant said. "The chores are done and we're all settled down for the night. Where were we before supper . . . talking about your son, old man? Yes, we got up through his schooling and into his fooling. Which brings me to one of those riddles a man finds about twice in his life. All the time I've been here, certain things have bothered me. Here's a pretty girl, married to your son and sleeping alone on a cot. That's no way for young married folks to act. It makes me wonder why Tony got married."

Old Casper was refreshed by food and coffee, just enough to dull his caution. He glared scornfully at Rachel and spoke his thought:

"He married for love . . . and look what it go him!"

"Father," Tony said curtly.

"You be still," Conant said. "You ain't old enough for these serious conversations. We're discussing marriage, and nothing is more serious."

"It sure as hell ain't," old Casper said fervently. "I told him—"

"I bet you did," Conant said. "Before he tied the hitch."

"You bet I did—"

"And I can guess what you told him," Conant said. "You being a good father and all, wanting a fine match for your only child. You told him he was too young, he ought to wait, think it over . . . didn't you?"

Old Casper's temper had gotten the best of him, released rancorous thoughts better kept under lock and key. Conant had led him down so many blind alleys he forgot to think before he spoke. He began with "—yes, and no dowry," and caught his tongue and mumbled, "something like that."

"You're a liar," Conant said pleasantly. "You were out here on this hog ranch without a woman. When he brought her home you probably split your pants with joy. Somebody to cook and wash and sew and lie to . . . hell, if he'd brought home a goat that could do the work you'd been just as happy. And then she broke a leg and I'll bet somebody had to hold down your gunhand to keep you from treating her like a horse or cow—"

"That's a lie," old Casper said hotly. "I never said or thought anything like that. I just—!"

"Yes," Conant said. "What did you just do, old man?"

"Climbing rocks," old Casper spit. "Acting like a damn kid. Busted her leg, now she can't have children, she—"

"I figured we'd get down to brass tacks," Conant said. "That's a mighty interesting statement, old man."

"It's true!"

"Is it?" Conant said. "Rachel, how many in your family?"

"Please—" she said.

"How many?"

"Eleven, señor."

"Eleven!" Conant said admiringly. "And how many in your wife's family, old man?"

"Fourteen," old Casper said. "But they ain't got nothin'—"

"And you," Conant said. "How many brothers and sisters did you claim?"

"Two, I guess."

"Why, we've got a real debate," Conant said. "Here's a woman about twenty years old, comes from a big healthy family, marries a strong young man, and busts her leg . . . and you claim a broken leg has stopped her from having children? Tony, I reckon you're a normal human being. You ain't no koshare, I don't think, although you'd make a pretty good clown in some respects. But we've got to get right down to bedrock with something as serious as this. When did you stop trying to have children, Tony?''

"You have no right—!" Tony said miserably.

"I'd say about two years," Conant mused. "Maybe longer. I'll bet the old man mounted his rostrum and declared, by God, that she couldn't bear a child, and you listened to those words of gospel and turned her out to pasture. . . . Well, jumping Jesus, look at her! There's nothing wrong with her. Just because some horse doctor set her bones a little crooked you think that changed everything else in a pretty, healthy girl? Old man, it seems to me you conveniently forgot that having babies is a two-way proposition. Maybe it ain't her fault at all—"

"No!" old Casper roared. "My son is—"

"I'll just bet he is," Conant said. "Here he spent that first afternoon advising me where to go and who to see, and telling me how he wore out the seat of his pants riding all over the valley collecting that female information. But has he got anything to show for that? . . . No, I can see he ain't. Now that's funny after two years. Yes, I could prove it to you, old man. I'll give her a baby . . . think I can't?''

Old Casper glared at him in helpless rage, and that rage vanished suddenly. Old Casper said, "I'll take that bet."

"You will?"

"Yes, by God," old Casper said with righteous innocence. "Now don't get me wrong—"

"Oh no!"

"I know it's a bad thing to say," old Casper said, "because I mean a good deal to Rachel—"

"You?" Conant said.

"Sure I do—"

"Old man," Conant said, "you mean nothing to her. You never did."

"Now don't you say that."

"She looks a hole through you," Conant said. "Don't you see how she feels about you? You're a damned old fool and just to know you proves it. But you'd bet, sure you would, and I don't notice Tony shouting objections. Maybe he knows more about his innards than you do. Maybe he put her out on that cot because he was ashamed of himself. Not that she caught on, I doubt that, but it makes sense to me. So you'd bet on it, old man?"

"You're fooling with me," old Casper said weakly.

"I don't fool, old man."

"But you can't be serious?" old Casper said.

"Why not?" Conant said lightly. "In a way I owe you something. And like you reminded me, here I am two years in Santa Fe and don't I feel almighty bad about that unnatural state of affairs? Put it on the line, old man. I'll cover your bet and pay off if and when, seeing we'll have to wait a while on the verdict."

"Father," Tony said harshly. "He is making you a fool!"

"Him?" Conant laughed. "I'm thirty years late to take that blame, Tony. But you've got nothing to say about this. You reneged a long time ago. . . . But never mind the money, chalk, or marbles. I'll just take Rachel for a *pasear* in the moonlight."

Listening, watching him, it seemed to Rachel Casper that he spoke in innocence, that any evil intended was outside of him a forgotten part of the inner whole created by them all. He prodded the old man while Tony suffered visibly and gave her darting, imperious looks. But she had seen her husband suffer in many ways, all foolishly selfish and leading directly to winning some cheap advantage over father, wife, or chance woman.

"Yes, sir," Conant said cheerfully. "Get some fresh air and moonlight."

When he untied her and boosted her erect, pushed her across the room, she glanced at Tony. Lamplight was cut off by their moving bodies, then flashed yellow clear on Tony's face. Their eyes met for one moment and she saw his darken with anger; but deep within the familiar outrage was a new anger, a kind of crazy pride for her that she had not seen in nearly three years. It was almost as if he suddenly saw a woman, not an ugly cripple with a barren womb. But even if he looked and raged inwardly, what did it mean? Some things came too late for anyone.

"Step out," Conant said. "What's the matter?"

"Nothing, señor."

She had taken two peyote buttons, all that remained to her after cutting and grinding the others into powder. She wished for more to bring her vision, or peace, or strength to accept the unknown.

"Good night all," Conant said.

He pushed her through the door and she wondered, as a girl might, for she was still a girl, what it would do to her. It had been so long she could not remember the act or the thoughts and feelings and hopes of the act. She did not know.

Conant laughed softly as he led her from the house into the blue darkness and clean wind; behind them the lamp cast yellowness through the doorway across the dust. Conant guided her around the chicken shed along the middle slope where tall grass fighting upward from the bottoms withered against the downward onslaught of sage and chamiso. She trembled when he pushed her down and dropped beside her, and that angered him. He wanted to explain that he meant no harm, his cruelty was centered on old

Casper and Tony, a means to an end; but the gentle words were not easily spoken. The best he could offer was the bluntness of truth.

"They don't care, Rachel."

"I know, señor."

"If it would cinch their staying healthy," Conant said, "they'd see you die. You know that?"

"Perhaps," she said.

"I didn't bring you out here for that," Conant said. "They think so but they don't count. I had enough of their faces and lies. I need fresh air."

"Yes, señor."

"Don't go meek on me," he said. "Don't look down, look up! You're as good as anybody. Remember that."

"I try."

"Well, you keep trying," Conant said forcefully. "And you talk if you want to. All the time they were blabbing I kept thinking you had forgot how. That's not good for you."

"If you wish," she said.

"You cold?"

"No, señor."

"Then stop shivering," Conant said irritably. "Now first off, I want a straight answer from you about something. I've got to leave tomorrow night. If that whisky-maker from Talpa don't see them by noon, will he come looking?"

"Yes," she said. "By nightfall."

"Which gives me around twenty hours leeway," Conant said. "Plenty but for one thing—they know where I'm heading."

"Yes," she said. "West, then to Mexico."

"Not that it matters," Conant said, "but the first thing they'll do is turn the whole shebang after me."

Warning touched her, fear moved softly. She tried to change his thoughts. "But, señor. Must you go south? Can you go to no one here?"

"Me?"

"But surely someone is your friend . . . someone remembers?"

"Once I knew a good many of the boys," Conant said moodily, "and some girls too. Over in Moreno, in Cimarron and Springer. Not now. It makes you wonder, the way things change when a man's gone two years. That's time enough to make everything different. I can't chance it over there—be like a foreign land. They'd like to see me again. Oh yes! I'm worth a thousand dollars to a bunch of tinhorn sports."

"No one," she said softly. "That is very lonely."

"You ought to know," Conant said.

His fingers probed blindly into the grass, snapped the stems and twisted them like a boy making cat cradles. They shared the same emotion and experience of loneliness with such closeness that it ceased to be the language of silence and gave her voice an almost forgotten gift of words. Loneliness was nothing to happy people; it never entered their minds or affected their lives. But with them it was shared; and when two separates touched, the sharing created a false closeness. It made her ask a question better unsaid.

"Would you do it again, señor?"

"You mean, kill them guards?"

"Yes."

"No living man can answer that question," Conant said. "I don't know . . . I just don't know. It's done, it can't be changed."

"What will you do with us?" she asked.

"I've been lucky," Conant said thinly. "Nobody stopping by, not much time till tomorrow night. . . . I can make the river and cross over by next morning. I'm not worried about them getting loose. They shot their wad. I don't want to hurt you but I've got to tie you the same way. . . . You sure somebody will come by?"

"Oh yes," she said. "My friend—"

"What . . . what friend?"

"Not a whisky-maker," she said. "I have a friend—" her voice was proud. "He comes when they are gone."

"Then I was wrong," Conant said. "All the time you—"

"Oh no," she said. "Not that kind. An old man, a Ute who lives with the Pueblos, a medicine man. Some say he is related to my grandfather. He will come on Saturday, near sunset."

"They don't know about him?"

"I do not tell them," she said.

"Twenty hours," he said wonderingly. "That Ute will come, they spill the beans, and that's it."

"But if you cross the river," she said, "they cannot find you."

"The odds favor me," Conant said. "But I can't put trust in odds from here on out."

"Then I know what you think," she said.

"Forget it," Conant said harshly. "It won't concern you."

"You would kill them?" she asked.

"I don't know yet."

"But if you kill them," she said, "what of me? I will be alive to talk."

"I don't kill women," he said. "There's always a limit. No, I better not say that. Nothing is certain. I might change. I don't know."

"But I must tell," she said. "If you leave me and others come."

"Forget it," he said. "I told you nothing is settled. I'll know in the morning."

"How, señor?"

He laid the rifle aside and turned her until they faced in the grass. He moved his hands over her shoulders and arms. "I can't take a chance," he said. "You might have slipped a knife out here."

"No," she said.

He moved her nearer and searched the small of her back, her thighs and hips, handling her impersonally, no violence in his hands. Her face in the night was pale, her eyes dark and her mouth shaped in fear. His fingers touched her hair and cupped the white oval of her face.

"No knife," he said.

"No."

It came over them naturally, like wind and rain and darkness, without words or movements native to the act. He came upon her and she took him, both in weariness and forgotten desire, with loneliness a third bedfellow until they drove him far away.

"Lay still," old Casper said. "You'll choke."

"He is out there—!" Tony said.

"By God," old Casper said. "I hope he keeps her all night and forgets what he's thinking about."

"My wife!" Tony said.

"Oh, shut up," old Casper said. "If I hadn't talked my head off, you'd have a knife in you right now—"

"No."

"Oh yes," old Casper said. "You're not thinking straight. Don't you see what's worrying him?"

Tony rolled over and stared at his father in the lamplight.

"No more advice," he said coldly. "Never again. We
tried, yes, and we failed. That was by us, and for us.
There was no need to give her like a dirty piece of silver."

"Gratitude," old Casper whined. "All these years and
now you treat me this way. . . . What the hell are you so
excited over her for? I'm thinking about us!"

Tony turned his head away. His father was shriveling,
but he had begun to grow, a terrible and vague feeling,
like a bellyache that came and went and was not understood. But it had started in him. Too late, he thought, too
late for the great fool he had been.

". . . listen to me," old Casper was saying, talking on
and on, unable to stop his threadbare hopes. "We still got
a chance, don't cross him, don't even look the wrong way,
let me handle it, I'll do the talking, he's got to leave us
like this, I'm not sure he's really thinking of killing us but
I can't tell, I just can't figure him out. If Joe comes on
Saturday afternoon we can get to town and tell them . . .
that ought to be worth part of the money if they get him,
now remember—"

"Shut up!" Tony said.

Furious anger shook him, mocked the foolish greed of
a man who took all things for granted and was brought to
comeuppance when someone found value in an unused
possession he had discarded long ago . . . but kept, oh
yes, to cook and sew and sweep. He thought of Conant
outside with Rachel, and cursed the frightened old man
who tried to exorcise death with futile words. Sleep came
at last and he welcomed it; for like himself, all his dreams
were childish; they dipped one toe into the safe shallows
of life. But tonight those dreams wrenched and battered

him, gave him no peace. He jerked against the rawhide hondo that chaffed his neck and cut his breath.

". . . our only chance," old Casper said for the tenth time. "She's our only chance."

"It is very late," she said. "You must not sleep."

"Not sleeping," Conant mumbled, holding her. "Just tired . . . so damn tired and I knew it before. I'm sorry."

"No," she said. "It is me. I am too ignorant for you."

"Ignorante?" he smiled.

"Si."

"Not you," he said. "Both of us."

For that was how it came to them through all the night, both wanting to give and then take, both coming with the same handicaps—weariness and innocence. There was no real difference in them. The years had made them true innocents and, as such, they could be forgiven a first time . . . but this was the end. They had found and released a forgotten part of themselves, and the wish for life which ran like steel throughout all procreation was strengthened and revived. There was no love between them, that could not be, nor would the night be remembered in any term of tenderness or longing. He had taken her but her surrender was not weakness; it was new-found strength.

"So damn tired," he said again.

"We must go in."

"Yes," Conant said. "It always comes to that."

He helped her stand and led her across the yard in the smoky darkness of three o'clock on a cool May morning. They returned to the musty smells and yellow lamplight; the night was fading, the hours dropped away from them. He took her to the cot and shook his head when she moved to lie down.

"You want to sleep?"

"No," she said, shy now, uncertain, but only of herself, not of him or the men on the floor.

"Then stay up," he said. "It's easier."

He tied her ankles to the posts, slipped her wrists behind her back, lashed them against her body. She could rest against the wall; it was much better than lying flat.

"Got to do this," he said.

"No matter."

"Well—"

He turned away to old Casper, to Tony, and checked their knots. Tony looked up, eyes lidded, unable even then to conceal the hatred. Conant said, "Sour grapes, eh?" and walked to the table. He laid the rifle with its muzzle pointing directly at the doorway, placed his hands upon the forearm and breech, right hand shaping over hammer and trigger. In a little while he had to face the chores and the meal. But not now. Just to lay his head on the oily metal, close his eyes, was all that mattered.

"Rachel," he said.

"Yes, señor."

"Wake me just before light," he said. "Gives me an hour."

"Not that much," she said.

"Whenever it's time." He raised his head a moment and looked at her. "Will you do it?"

"Yes, señor."

"I'll trust you," he said.

Then he dropped into rest that was not true sleep but a passage through time with his mind still worrying the problem. Instinct warned that exhaustion was as near as skin itself, that his body could not stave off collapse much longer. Well, he thought, today and tonight, he must get through them somehow. The night was gone—and now his mind skipped—and all between them had to be forgotten.

105

But the memory of gentleness would linger, the unfamiliar gifts of timidity and wonder and thankfulness. Love? . . . He refused the meaning of the word, if love had meaning in the words of men. He had never known it in the way it must be, not through all the years spent in the dingy corners where momentary pleasure masqueraded boldly as love and served a full purpose because he needed no more than masquerade. Now he would never find it. No, he thought, there was one way. If love came through death, as someone once explained, then he might feel it at last. But not before killing was done and he had finished with death; and when could that be? He was not finished. He could never call it quits, the way he went now, until he paid the last debt himself.

"Stop it," he said in sleep. "Make up your mind!"

"Rachel!" old Casper hissed.

"Yes."

"What's he goin' to do?"

"I do not know."

"But he told you something?"

"Nothing."

"You can handle him," old Casper said. "I know you can, girl."

"Be still," Tony said.

Old Casper glared at his son. "Rachel!"

"Leave her in peace," Tony said.

"He does not bother me," she said calmly.

"Are you well?" Tony asked.

"Yes."

"Did he—?"

"Yes," she said. "There is no reason to talk."

How true, he thought. It was strange to remember how few words they had spoken in the past. Not a great amount of talk was necessary to their marriage. They could get along on three words a day if the feeling of respect and love existed. He had been ignorant of both, and now he felt that emptiness. He lay on his side with the rawhide choking his throat and stared at her without hope.

"You are right," Tony said, "but ignore my father. He is not to be obeyed."

"No," she said. "Or you."

"Or me," he agreed dully. "Protect yourself. I know what he will do."

He turned painfully and shut his eyes to the rising wonder of the shape and feel of death; and thinking in that way he was sharply aware of her again. He saw her as she was, had always been, and in that strange way of their kind he was proud of her.

She saw his eyes before he turned and they told her what she knew at last: she was not ugly. Only in Tony's eyes, her young beauty dulled by her leg, persuaded by his father, was she ugly. That had been his blindness these three years; and equally her blindness for giving up so easily. It had been in her hands from the start, to do with as she chose. Beauty worked outward in a woman, moved and touched the man who loved her. When the feeling was destroyed he saw only the image of his own shame and disappointment . . . if he was immature, if he had brought shallowness with his first love.

But men matured in time; it was not his fault, but their blood, that made such men as he slow unto death. The veriest fool was not hopeless. The wastrel could awaken, the rake could change and use one bed alone. It came from the woman to the man and it must be real at last, and always one must be the stronger . . . and she was far stronger. She knew that now. It must be that way if they

107

salvaged anything at all . . . no, she thought, that was not quite true. If she *wished* to salvage anything. If she looked now, around the corner of the years, and found anything worth saving, worth returning to.

"Rachel!" old Casper whimpered.

She looked at him and smiled. He would never change. He was measuring death by his own fear and discomfort, and she knew you could not measure death. It was too deep and wide to compare with anything they knew. Poor old fool, she thought, clinging to the last rag-taggle shreds of his life as they blew away on unfeeling wind.

"Rachel!"

"Old man," she said, "be still!"

Old Casper squeaked in terror. He stared as if he saw a ghost, heard a devil. She had never spoken to him in that way. No woman had in all his life. He had never needed a woman's help. Now he wanted life, he wanted assurance from any hole or corner, but he had not expected this. His mouth fell open and she stared him down.

"Be still, old man. I am thinking."

"Yes, Rachel," old Casper said. "You do that . . . you can help us, he'll listen to you now—"

Listen to her now? The old man did not learn with time. Conant would listen to no one, ever, not her or any woman.

"Rachel?" old Casper whispered, persistent as a fly. "Can you do it?"

"Please," she said. "I am thinking."

"Is there a way—?"

"Perhaps," she said, "but I am thinking of you. Are you worth saving, father-in-law?"

"Father," Tony Casper said. "There is no way. For the last time, shut your foolish mouth!"

* * *

Conant lay upon his rifle as gray dawn came slowly from the east. Sleeping, dreaming, he did not hear the horse trot upstream from the west, turn off the creek trail, ascend the path into the yard. The horse stopped before the door and the rider got down, grunting with fatigue, and came slack-hipped into the doorway. He blinked against the yellow light, rubbed one dirty hand over his eyes, and coughed.

"Hey," he called. "Casper . . . Tony!"

Conant heard the voice and raised his head an inch. He stared mistily toward the door and heard the gasp as old Casper woke in the darkness that concealed his body.

"Shoot him!" old Casper roared. *"Shoot him!"*

"What?"

"The table," old Casper shrieked. *"The table!"*

Conant woke as the rider wheeled, clawed at his belt, and blinked into the lamplight. Conant's right eye was on line with his rear sight; his thumb cocked the hammer and he fired along that plane without moving, the rifle bucking against his cheek. He leaped backward from the chair, levered the Winchester frantically, and saw the rider bring a revolver waist high, falter as the bullet struck, and fall.

"Shoot him!" old Casper sobbed. "Oh . . . shoot—"

Conant ran as the revolver dropped and the rider folded inward. He was dead, taken by a chance and lucky shot through the heart, and he did not move when Conant knelt and touched his chest. The horse snorted to the echo of the shot and Conant, leaping outside in one great bound, swung his rifle in an arc and expected the worst. The yard was empty.

"Dear God!" he said, unbelieving.

He caught the bit and dragged the horse across the yard into the shed, casting glances on all sides as he ran, afraid his shot was heard by unseen men. He pushed the horse into a stall and crouched in the shed door, watching the creek bottom, the slopes, the distant skyline clearing in the dawn. The black horse came from the creek, attracted by the stranger, ran around into the corral, and through the back door into the shed.

Conant closed both doors and worked feverishly, pulling down hay, pouring oats, carrying gear from the pegs. He saddled the black horse, tossed the saddlebags on his shoulder, and stepped outside. He closed the door behind him, wedged it with a stick, and ran to the house. Whatever happened now, however the day came and was used, he was prepared for night.

Old Casper was crying at the closeness of death. Conant had no time to give orders; the nearness of day was bursting within him. He caught the dead man by the collar and dragged him from the house across the yard to the chicken shed. The chickens rushed crazily for the wall holes, beating their wings, crowing in alarm, kicking up dirt and feathers that smelled as dry and bitter as the fear in his mouth. He laid the dead man in the corner under the smudged roost poles and saw the star gleaming silver-bright on the vest. He took the holster and belt, and looked for the first and last time at the face. Very dark, full and round, a man in his forties. Conant ducked through the low door and ran for the house. He was always running now, it seemed; he could not stop.

Old Casper was still crying, wrapped tightly in a ball beneath the window. Conant buckled the holster belt around his waist, found the revolver, a .38 Colt, and seated it against his thigh.

"Turn around, old man," he said. "There's nobody else can hear you."

He stood in the doorway and watched sunlight break above the peaks, chase the last shadows from the land. If

110

the deputy had come from a guard mount on the river, riding into town, he had a little time. If the deputy was riding from town en route to the river, there was more time. But alone . . . his luck ran on, thinner and thinner, but still holding true. He faced them with his question.

"You know him?"

"Yes," Tony said coldly. "He was my friend."

"Regular deputy or signed on?"

"Regular," Tony said. "His name was Carlos Valerio. He had a wife and five children."

"Never mind the history," Conant said harshly.

"Pardon me," Tony Casper said stiffly. "You are right, of course. It does not matter now."

He looked quickly at Tony and moved to the table. Had his thoughts shown so clearly in a few words, in his face standing here in the half-light? If Tony knew, then she knew, even the old man who had rolled over and stared, he must have an inkling. Conant had slept undecided, woke to kill again, and when the old man shrieked, "Shoot him . . . shoot him!" it was decided for him. That and the second horse. The horse made all the difference. Now he could do it as planned, where before he saw no way, no hope. He snuffed out the lamp and placed the rifle on the table.

"Looks like a hot day," he said. "And a long one."

Seven

SUNRISE HAD RACED HIM AND EXPOSED HIM WHILE HE carried wood and water, but still his luck held true. He stood eating in the doorway and they watched his every move, but he had no thought for them. His consciousness searched far into the vast emptiness he must enter in twelve hours' time. His mind asked the unanswerable questions: Where were the posses? Which crossing was safe—Taos Junction, Tres Piedras, or Red River? Would they call off the hunt today?

It was worse than roulette. A man played red or black and lost only money; tonight he would bet his life on two to one odds.

"I'd like to be a mouse," he said wistfully. "Skedaddle into that courthouse and put my whiskers in the crack, listen to that high muck-a-muck from Santa Fe, all those marshals and three-dollar-a-day manhunters. Find out where those boys are guarding the river and if they're bringing up the Indian trackers from the south. But hell, it don't matter. Somebody might come by here just the same and put me in the bind. Then all the crossings could be open for the good it'd do me. Yes, somebody in that courthouse is going to be judge and jury on old J.S. Conant, Esquire. He'll say the word and they'll all pop. An' they must be getting awful tired by now. I wonder if they feel like me. . . ."

His body cried soundlessly for rest, an end to endless punishment. Food no longer helped and coffee brought a weak resurgence; smoking was meaningless. Nothing tasted good in his parched throat. He wanted to kick off his boots and rub his aching feet but he dared not today, for he might be forced to run and ride at any moment.

"What are you all doin' in there?" he said angrily. "All of you law-abiding, reward-hunting bastards?"

The weary men gathered round the sheriff's rolltop desk in the courthouse. They drank coffee and ate sandwiches and watched the U.S. marshal from Santa Fe leaf through the skimpy reports and toss the soiled sheets aside.

"Hogwash!" he said. "Two hundred men and not a sign of him."

The county sheriff drummed his thick fingers on the desk and obeyed an old rule handed down by his father: keep your teeth on your tongue. He was not paid to advise high officials. He would speak when spoken to.

"Well," the U.S. marshal said, "what do you think?"

"He's holed up," the sheriff said.

"Where?"

"Somewhere around here," the sheriff said. "That's why there's no use looking this way."

"What would you do?"

"Pull in my horns," the sheriff said. "Smoke him out."

"I agree," the marshal said. "Send word to the river, tell them to come in and don't make a secret of it. The

Indians'll be here tonight. Maybe he'll make his move then. . . ."

As the messenger trotted from the plaza into Ranchitos Road, heading for the three posses that worked the river from camps at Taos Junction, Tres Piedras, and Red River, those men gathered sluggishly about their breakfast fires. They had hunted fruitlessly through the side canyons and arroyos and forests, beaten the river banks in the gorge bottom, looked under every sage-brush, chamiso, and juniper that laid enough shadow to hide a man; and in all that great expanse they found no sign, no track. Now they waited on the day's order and sensed the command long before the messenger arrived. . . .

On the Talpa ridge the whisky-maker and his son cleaned their ancient copper tubes and pots, stacked charcoal and wood, prepared for the following day.

"Think they'll come?" the son asked.

"Better," his father grunted.

"I could ride down and make sure, eh?"

"Hah!" his father said. "And leave this work to me? You stay here. He owes us a day and if he's not here by noon I'll go down and cut off his . . ."

One thing can tip a balance. Rain, snow, wind, rock slide; a thrown shoe, a faulty rifle, one defective shell. Or the human element.

The Indian trackers employed by the territorial government had been working on a cow thief case when the order caught them deep in the mountains between Reserve and Datil. Now they were ending another long journey, coming slowly up the narrow gauge line from Santa Fe to Taos Junction depot. They would detrain and ride the last leg across the river to Taos, receive their orders, and begin another chase. Five of them, the finest trackers in the territory, quiet men who sat in the caboose and watched the land slip past the windows.

They were the human element. Life or death waited patiently behind those pseudo-solemn faces.

"Yes," Conant mused on. "I wonder what they're doing?"

He dared not sit in the chair, already his head drooped, his body cried for sleep. He looked up, saw the moving figure, and leaped backward into deeper room shadow. The rider came swiftly, glanced upward at the yard, and went on downstream without a second look. Conant ran to the bedroom window and watched him out of sight. The thin wire of reason grew tighter within him, approached the edge of endurance. He clung to sanity with words.

"Is he the answer to the maiden's prayer? Ugly-looking cuss, but if he brings those boys back to town he's sure an angel."

He came from the bedroom, rubbing his bristly jaw, and caught fiercely at that commonplace.

"Real ungentlemanly of me," he said. "I can't meet company looking like a tramp."

He built up the fire and heated water, soaped his face and stropped the old man's razor. He shaved by touch, drawing blood from a dozen tiny cuts, guiding the razor across cheek and jaw, skirting the bulging Adam's apple. He did not use the mirror. He wanted no confirmation of the face he would see. If he looked, he might give up. His fingers described the shape of skin pulled smaller over bones, the gauntness that thrust his nose outward between his eyes.

"A sight for sore eyes," he said. "How do I look, Rachel?"

"As you are," she said.

"Now you're being polite," he said. "Tony, how do I look to you?"

"Shaved," Tony said.

"You're dodging the issue," Conant said. "Old man, what do you see?"

Old Casper's eyes were closed, his face was flabby with ever-growing terror. Through the meal and the sound of Conant bringing wood and water, he refused to recognize the final truth. His face was shapeless now, but the day would unwind and his skin grow taut, his eyes open despite his fear.

"Well, old man?"

"The same," old Casper said.

"How can you tell," Conant said, "plopped down there with your eyes shut? . . . Did I hurt your feelings, you want to talk?"

"No," old Casper said. "Please . . . no!"

"Why not?" Conant said. "There's nothing else to do. If you can't talk, you must be sick. Rachel, you think he's sick?"

"Yes, señor."

"Too bad," Conant said. "I'm no doctor."

He sat gingerly in the chair and watched the old man's head roll in helpless agony. He would not speak the words and so far they had not found the courage to ask point-blank . . . not the old man, at least. He was not sure of Tony. He had forgotten them during breakfast and the early hours, but the time had come to make his plans.

He drew the little .32 from his hip pocket and spun the cylinder. He had put off the final plan too long; it was foolish waiting till nightfall. A blanket to muffle the sound, he thought, and the little .32. Two shots . . . then take the saddlebags and the girl to the shed, mount up, and ride.

"No fancy trimmings," he said aloud. "Simple and neat."

"Why—?" old Casper said, his voice frail.

"Why what?" Conant said.

He pocketed the .32 and took up the rifle; it had taken the old man all that time to face the truth and find his voice. They watched Conant silently, and now old Casper had released their thoughts.

"What?" Conant said. "Speak up, old man."

"Don't keep looking at me that way," old Casper said. "Say it!"

"Old man," Conant said gently, "I don't mean to look at you any way but decent. I'm not trying to be mean."

"You're going to kill us," old Casper said. "Kill us! Go on, say it, please say it—"

"Damn it, old man!" Conant said. "What's the use of saying what we all know—"

"Why?" old Casper said. "Why does it happen to me?"

"Because humans are such funny animals," Conant said. "We make our own troubles, old man, and that kind is always the worst."

"Say it!" old Casper repeated.

"All right," Conant said. "If it'll make you feel any better, yes, that's the way it stands. Both of you, tonight after super."

"But why?" old Casper said brokenly. "Why do you need to?"

"It won't do no good to explain," Conant said patiently. "My reasons won't make sense to you because you ain't me. But they do to me. It's me against all of you, old man. I'll tell you why, slow and plain, and just one time.

I'm leaving here after dark. You know where I'm going, the only way I can chance it, west to the river. Now from tonight until tomorrow afternoon I've got twenty hours more or less to bank on before somebody comes in here. That's not enough time because you'd talk and they'd be after me like scat. I need two days, three with luck. If nobody can tell them I was even here, or where I headed, or when I left out, it stands to reason I just might get a three-day start before they're organized.''

"No," old Casper said. "We won't—"

"That's gone by the boards," Conant said. "All the fussing and fuming, the lying. No more room for argument. You brought this to a head at—let's see, just past ten o'clock—when you'd been better off to try and forget. We've got to get through the day. It's no easier on me than you. But that's your worry, you handle it. I can't help."

"It ain't right," old Casper whispered.

"Father," Tony said. "Be still!"

"You see," Conant said. "Take a lesson from your son, old man. You told me you brought him up. You ought to be proud of the job. He learned more than you figured. He's not ramming his nose in the dirt and asking silly questions—"

"No," Tony Casper said, "but I would talk."

"Sure, go on, Tony."

"Am I to understand," Tony said, "that Rachel goes with you?"

"Yes," he said. "She goes with me."

"But you will not keep her?"

"Not long."

"You think you can make it," Tony said. "You truly think that, Conant?"

"If you mean," Conant said, "can I tell you how I'll make it, have I got a sure-fire plan, hell no, nobody could.

I'll just start and keep going. I know they'll send the trackers after me sooner or later, but they've got to find the right trail and start it. That takes time in this country. Give me three days and I'll lose 'em all.''

"You will travel by night?''

"Most likely.''

"But they will follow day and night.''

"Slow at night,'' Conant said. "And I'll keep going by day too, when there's good cover—trees and canyons and the like. No, they won't get me from behind. In front? Who knows, eh? At the railroads and along the border it could happen. But not from behind. Not on your good horse, Tony.''

"How is the other horse?''

"Fair,'' he said.

"Rachel does not ride well,'' Tony said.

"That's no worry,'' Conant said. "She won't need to ride far.''

"That is how I have thought,'' Tony said. "Will you promise to bury her deep.''

"What . . . stop joking!''

"I do not joke,'' Tony said seriously. "You must promise.''

"Man,'' he said, "I won't hurt her. I'll turn her loose.''

"You swear it?''

"No,'' he said. "I'll swear to nothing, never again, not even the sun rising. But I won't hurt her.''

"Swear it!''

"Oh, go to hell,'' he laughed mirthlessly. "If you don't believe me, who cares. It won't matter to you anyway.''

"But it matters now,'' Tony said softly. "Today . . . what is left to today.''

"Son—'' old Casper said.

"Be still,'' Tony said. "Face it like a man.''

Then old Casper knew he would die. He had refused to accept the truth when Carlos was shot before his eyes, but it was upon them all now and he could not offer one word, one thought, one feeling, that spoke of life.

"Yes," he murmured to himself.

He saw the truth so late he had no time to make his terms with life and face death. He stared through the doorway at the mountains and the sky, all the land he had ignored so many blind years and saw now with exquisite pain. He looked and the land fell away, as if he stared through a reversed spyglass and saw it all far distant, so beautiful it was unbearable. It was sudden color to a blind man, overpowering and sad to a point transcending tears. There was no hope, no return. He saw too late, and seeing, knew a strange thing and wondered if his son felt that way too. This was happening to them, he saw and felt it, and he seemed to be separated from his body; he stood aside with no connection with or feeling for the flesh. It was like death before the heart stopped; it was a foretaste of heaven or hell, without bliss or agony.

". . . then I must believe you, Conant," Tony was saying. "I will believe you."

"That's the spirit," Conant said. "You hang onto that, Tony."

"By God," Tony said. "I can't find anything else."

"Ain't it enough?" Conant asked.

"It has to be," Tony said, and shrugged. "What's got into me, eh? I am thinking too much."

"About what?" he asked.

"Oh, me," Tony Casper said. "I keep thinking there's something wrong with this somewhere, or maybe it's me. Did I ever know anything, did I ever believe in anything? Do I leave anything behind? Next year who will remember and speak my name? And the next year, eh, all the years—

1901, '02, '03, '13, '30—by God, I tell you, I don't know but I don't like it. I had all that time coming to me, you know, and now I'll never get to spend it. What a dirty trick!" He looked up at Conant and laughed. "Don't you think it is a dirty trick?"

"I've got to agree," Conant said. "I felt the same way for two years."

"And you escaped?"

"So far," he said. "So far."

"Listen, hombre," Tony said. "If you make it to Mexico, you think of me, eh? Think how I'll miss thirty years and how you better live them twice as big for me. . . . Now there's a promise to make and keep."

"If I make Mexico," Conant said. "I can't promise I'll live 'em up any bigger, but they'll sure go fast."

"Good," Tony said. "When you drink, drink for two. When you eat, eat for two. When you—" he looked at Rachel and shook his head. "I sound crazy. What does it matter? Who cares . . . ?"

Rachel listened to their words and watched Tony's face. He was not acting but he had changed so quickly. He had lost hope of life and somehow found the courage to face death. He was not the man she had married, the man who courted her, made her feel love, led her to the altar and into this house. He was not the man who ran wildly to her aid when she fell, carried her to town, hovered frantically while the doctor set her leg. He was not the man who, weeks later, pushed her into the kitchen and rode all the night trails in the valley. Oh, he was the same in those ways, for no man could entirely throw off old habits as a snake changed skin. But he was changing before her eyes in other ways, and he touched her with that strength. He was not acting. He was about to die and had no reason to worry over her, to ask Conant for promises . . . unless he truly cared.

She was a simple person, inarticulate, with no depths of wisdom. All she could do was sense out the truth. She tried to judge her husband with her simple tools, the mind that reasoned painfully, the heart that felt instinctively but was sorely handicapped because it had never known true love. She looked at the man who had lain with her through the night, the man who had shown her tenderness and great desire, and now she felt the overwhelming irony: that Conant in sleeping with her had awakened her to love, but not with him. He had given her that and she, in return, could give him death.

Tony expected no miracle from her, but she knew a way, a chance. If the old Ute had spoken truth concerning peyote, there was a way. She closed her eyes and remembered the old Ute's words.

"Son," old Casper said. "I don't want to die."

"Who does?" Tony said.

"Can't we do nothin'?" old Casper asked.

"Yes," Tony said. "You can die with dignity."

Old Casper answered with complete honesty, "I don't know how," and shook his head in terror.

"Let him alone," Conant said. "He can't hear you, Tony."

"I know," Tony said softly. "Make it quick for him, eh?"

"Do my best," Conant said. "For you too."

She had learned that eight buttons taken during a night were safe. She could eat them at regular intervals and find release from pain and trouble. Nor need she fear the buttons would make her a slave to the custom. They were not habit-forming. She could live weeks on end without the need, take the buttons when she wished.

But there was another world of the peyote beyond her own. The old Ute had spoken gravely of that shadow land. He told how some men, in dire need, must pass far beyond the ordinary dosage of eight buttons. It was delicate business and he did not recommend such a trance. But if a man reached that time when he must forget completely or go mad, there was a way.

You could not chew enough buttons to bring about the trance. It was necessary to distill the peyote, condense a huge dose and swallow it quickly. Eight buttons gave one-third the required dose. Twenty-five buttons, distilled, must be swallowed. The best way was to cut and mince the buttons into powder, then steep that powder in a pot. The man must drink it all; then, depending on the individual, the trance would come within an hour and a half.

"What will it do to me?" she had asked.

The old Ute had smiled. Nothing was certain, but some results were predictable. A man lost interest in the world about him and entered his own. He was truly separated from all the life he knew. The angry man grew calm. The man who desired to move mountains suddenly did not care if all the flowers grew to treetop height and blocked his path.

"If I wished to strike someone," she had asked, "could I strike then?"

"Not you," the old Ute smiled. "I cannot say it would be so of all men. But you would not strike, no matter the depth of your hate. You would not care . . . most men do not care then."

He had told her no more. She repeated that knowledge and watched Conant. As the afternoon died and the time approached, she shrank from the terrible weight of making a decision. But she must decide, and soon. For, if she so decided, Conant must drink tea no later than six o'clock. Darkness came at seven-thirty. She had that much time before he took up the little .32.

"What is the time?" Tony asked.

"Five," Conant said. "You getting hungry?"

"Is it the custom," Tony said, "to eat before you die?"

"That's how they do it at Santa Fe," Conant said. "They hung a couple while I was there. I heard they could have anything they wanted that last meal."

"What a problem," Tony said, "for a man with much knowledge of food."

"I guess so."

"But not for me," Tony said.

"Why not?"

"I could ask," Tony said, "but how would you satisfy my wishes? All we have here—ham, beans, rice, coffee—"

"There is no coffee," Rachel said quietly.

"What?" Conant said.

"It is gone," she said. "But I have tea."

"Better'n nothing," Conant said. "Well, Tony, you better not yell for roast turkey or *cabrito* or anything fancy. Wish I had a drink for you."

"No matter," Tony said. "It will all taste bad."

"I'm not so damn hungry myself," Conant said.

"But why not? . . . You are not going to die."

"Maybe not tonight," Conant said. "I'm just not hungry."

"Because you will kill us?" Tony asked. "You have already killed three men. Two more, poof! What's the difference, one or a hundred."

"None when you figure it that way," Conant said flatly. "Except for one thing . . . I'm no killer."

"But you are, hombre," Tony said softly. "Don't you know that now? I have seen one killer before you—"

"Where?"

"At Questa," Tony said.

"How do you know what he was?"

"I saw it in the gambling room," Tony said. "He killed two men and I saw his eyes. They were like your eyes."

"Tony," Conant said, "you don't show good sense. Are you trying to hurry me, get me mad?"

"But you are mad," Tony laughed. "And what's the difference, now or after dark?"

"Maybe I'm crazy," Conant said. "An' a killer to boot, but we'll wait—"

He walked to the south window and looked up the long slope. He saw the first rider, then the others, a long string coming from the southwest with their pack horses. He stood at the window until they vanished, holding himself rigidly unconcerned. He went to the doorway and watched the creek bottoms, then untied Rachel and pointed to the stove.

"Ah," Tony said. "You have regained your appetite?"

"Some," Conant said. "Know why?"

"Please tell me."

"They're coming in," Conant said. "The bunch from Taos Junction just passed by. Know what that means? . . . They'll all be in from the river. And tonight! Think of it, just like I waltzed into the courthouse and give the order myself."

"You are very lucky," Tony said. "Now you can cross the river."

"You don't need to kill us now," old Casper said. "There ain't no reason—"

"It don't change a thing," Conant said, "and you know that! Rachel, hurry up with the grub."

He watched her move about the stove while he began the important work. He filled the saddlebags with food and extra clothing, checked his rifle and the dead man's Colt. He found a candle on the shelf and placed it in readiness for the night. The cooking smells touched his nose and made him eager, almost strong again, but as he waited he could not maintain the fable.

"Hurry it up," he said thickly.

"Yes, señor."

She moved deliberately over the stove, stirring the food, filling a teapot with boiling water and setting it aside to steep. The watch read six o'clock when she turned.

"Tony," he said. "You want to eat?"

"Thank you, no," Tony said.

"Old man?"

Old Casper stared piteously and Conant looked away from that dying face.

"Fill me a plate."

She brought the food and he tried to eat, but his mouth was sour. He forced a few swallows and pushed the plate away.

"Coffee," he said.

"No coffee," she said. "There is the tea, señor."

"Well, it better be hot," Conant said. "I can drink about two gallons."

The tea burned his tongue and was oddly bitter on the roof of his mouth. He sniffed the cup, drank again, and licked his chapped lips.

"Tastes funny."

"It is cheap tea," Rachel said. "Very bitter and strong."

"Worse'n Arbuckle's coffee," Conant said. "Can't be helped . . . you want some?"

"You will need it all," she said quietly.

"Yes," he said. "Go over there, Rachel."

He followed her to the cot and tied her hands securely in her lap. "Sorry," he said. "Got to do it until we leave out."

He returned to the table and filled his cup. He rolled a cigarette and smoked between gulps of tea, waiting for darkness and the bad part of leaving this house. He shook the teapot, poured the last cup that flowed muddy with the bottom residue, saw those soggy leaves and stems with uncanny lucidity.

"Wrong color," he said. "Must be the water."

He gagged on the last cup and swallowed it all in one gulp. Then he waited for the tea to clear his head, give him wakefulness, and half an hour later he felt the sensation clearly.

"Better'n coffee," he said in amazement. "Now how come I never knew that before?"

He smoked, and for the first time in days a cigarette had taste and smell in his throat. He stared at the cup, at steam rising from the kettle on the stove; and objects were changing subtly before his eyes as if he saw color where color had not existed in the past.

Soft light touched the stove with gold and turned to red. Conant closed his eyes and opened them to find blue marching over the walls, shimmering greenly on the stove. Everything had suddenly acquired new depth and brilliance of color. He sat in childlike wonder as the minutes passed, playing with the colors that his eyes saw in every adobe brick, on every board and piece of metal, in the very air.

The change in him, as time passed and dusk swept the sky, was not his new perception of color and object. Those impressions were intensified; he saw everything with new interest, but they did not matter. It was his will that changed within him.

Conant could not know how the will suffered a profound change when struck by a massive dose of peyote. A man suddenly did not care, saw no reason to do anything at all. The most important problems of the moment became unimportant. A man was not interested; he simply could not bother. He thought of better things. All the world around him seemed to become as it should be; but underneath, in some secret part of him, he sensed that something was wrong.

Still, it did not matter. Conant looked at them and was overcome with laughter at their strained faces, their unaccountable fear. Why should they be afraid?

Tony Casper could not believe his own eyes. Conant had a strange look and his voice was different, in the manner of an Indian chewing peyote during a ceremony. But where and how? It was not possible. He glanced quickly at Rachel and wished he dared to speak; and then Conant was speaking and all he could do was swallow his fear and hope that it was actually taking place.

"What's the matter?" Conant said. "Are you scared of something?"

Tony looked at him from the darkness and answered cautiously. "No, we are not afraid."

"No reason to be," he said. "None at all."

"Son," old Casper quavered. "He's crazy—"

"Be still," Tony said in a strained voice. "For the love of God, for one time in your life, be still—"

"But—"

"Yes," Conant said. "Don't bother us, old man. Can't

129

you see we're busy? We've got a lot to talk about . . . eh, Tony?"

"Yes," Tony said. "A great deal. What is in your mind, Conant?"

"Wait," Conant said.

He struck a match and lit the candle, dripped a blob of hot wax to hold it erect, and looked across the room with pleasure.

"Good light," he said. "Better'n the lamp."

He smoked and talked about places and people long forgotten. Night came on, darkness enveloped the house. Conant peered at the watch and spoke in amazement.

"Seven-thirty! . . . Where did the time go?"

"It goes," Tony said. "What did you say of that horse?"

"No matter," Conant said. "There is something else—"

"It is time to go," Rachel said softly.

"Where?" Conant asked.

"To go," she said. "I will need clothes to ride."

"Well, get them," Conant said. "Get them."

"In the bedroom," she said.

"That's where clothes ought to be," Conant said happily. "Go on, get them."

She entered the bedroom and gathered up levis, shirt, and jacket in her bound hands. When she returned to the doorway, Conant rose from the table with his rifle and the .32. He walked to the front door and back to the stove, then to her cot where he lifted a blanket. He turned and stared at old Casper in puzzlement; and the old man cried, one strangled sound, and fainted dead away.

"Got to do something," Conant said. "Know there's something—"

She stepped between Conant and Tony; and now she

had come to the moment and could not tell if it would work. She dared not go too far and ask him for the rifle, nor would she.

"It is time," she said. "We must go."

She touched his arm and turned him from them. His fingers grasped the saddlebags and he hung them over his shoulder. He walked with her into the darkness and looked upward at the sky.

"Something's wrong," he said. "Oh, hell, it don't matter."

"The horses," she said.

"That's it," he said. "The horses."

Crossing the yard, she saw his shoulders sag, heard the shuffle of his boots in the dust. He was weary unto death but she knew his feeling: His body had no weight, no weariness. They entered the shed where the horses stamped and nickered in impatience.

"Why, the poor devils," Conant said. "Not a lick to eat since morning."

"Untie me," she said firmly.

"What's the matter with me?" Conant said. "You can't ride that way . . . course you can't."

He untied her wrists and seemed to forget her presence. He pulled down hay, poured oats, stood patiently watching the horses eat. When they were done, he tightened the cinches and strapped the saddlebags on the black and shoved the rifle into the leather boot.

"We must go," she said.

"I know," Conant said. "If I could just remember—"

They led the horses from the shed and Conant helped her swing onto the brown and shortened the stirrups to fit her legs. He mounted the black horse and stared at the house and shook his head. He had forgotten something, but it did not matter.

131

"You ready?" he asked.

"Yes, señor," she said. "Where do we ride?"

"Oh, it don't matter," Conant said. "You got someplace to go?"

"You spoke of Taos Junction," she said.

"Why not?" Conant said merrily. "It's a fine night for a ride."

Eight

Tony Casper heard their voices as they rode past the house onto the slope and away in the night. He had no balance, lashed as he was, but he must rise and get his teeth into the thong that bound his neck to the door-post. Impossible before, with Conant in the room, it was possible now.

"Up!" he ordered himself. "Get up!"

He drove his body savagely. He worked his legs around, conscious of the thong, knowing if he slipped he might strangle before regaining slack. The fact that he could lie safely until someone came next day had vanished from his thoughts.

"The feet!" he said. "Underneath, you stupid bastard!"

His back mashed against the doorpost, his boot toes dug into the hard dirt. He pressed his fingernails into the post and tightened his thigh muscles. He lifted an inch, two inches, and fell.

"No!" he shouted.

Old Casper stirred and opened one eye. "Son . . . is this the way it—?"

"Wake up!" Tony said.

"Ain't we dead?" Old Casper asked.

133

"You are alive," Tony said. "Don't move, don't talk!"

He rose like a tight-strung bow, bent backward like an old man in the last throes of spinal disease. He pirouetted on his toes and pressed into the post, caught the thong in his teeth, and began chewing. His father was sobbing with the miracle of life, and those cries matched the rhythm of Tony's jaws as he bit into the salty rawhide thong. He chewed forever, it seemed, before the thong parted and he threw himself away from the doorpost and rolled on the floor.

He wrenched his body around until his hands pressed his father's mouth; and now old Casper needed no directions. He nuzzled like a dog, his teeth searched out knots and began tugging, pulling, chewing, twisting. Tony lay on his side, face in the dirt, and compressed his wrists with all his strength to give his father every tiny bit of slack. Old Casper loosened one knot, another, and suddenly Tony's hands were free.

He moved his arms forward and flat-handed himself toward the table like a legless cripple. He found the knife and slashed his leg thongs, leaped to his feet, and collapsed in an agony of knotted muscles and blood rushing through cramped veins and arteries. He crawled to his father, cut the neck thong, slashed the hands free, and dropped the knife.

"Wait!" old Casper cried.

Tony Casper ignored his father. He staggered from the house and crossed the yard to the creek trail. He ran like a drunken man, weaving, falling, until strength returned and he fled upstream toward the horse in his neighbor's barn, toward the town and the men waiting there.

Nine

DUST POWDERED THE GRASS BESIDE THE RIVER BRIDGE
and sifted between the loose planks when the horses
crossed in the dying night. From where they rode in the
gorge bottom, dwarfed by the wall, rising endlessly to the
rims, the sky appeared far beyond reach.

"We must stop here," she said.

"Why?" Conant asked.

"You are tired," she said. "You must eat."

Conant caught her reins and pulled the brown horse off
the trail into the shadow of the bridge.

"It's wore off now," he said. "You can't fool me no
more."

"I did not fool you," she said.

"No use arguing," he said. "Get down and drink . . .
and we'll have some talk."

While the horses drank and turned aside to nibble in the
grass, Conant glanced at the paling sky and laughed
harshly.

"Ought to be twenty miles west of here. How'd you do
it?"

"We rode very slow," she said. "We stopped to rest."

"Not that," he said. "What was it? I remember drinking the tea, even grabbing the blanket and getting all set to finish the job . . . and then she goes blank on me."

"Peyote," she said. "In the tea."

"And there was no killing?"

"No," she said. "You left them alive."

He went on his knees and thrust his head into the water, rose up to adjust his stirrups and check his cinch. He looked at her in wonder.

"I know about peyote," he said. "Saw an old buck eat some once. But you never handed me no ordinary dose."

"No," she said. "Twenty-five buttons in your tea."

"Hell," he said. "Tony's loose by now. I've got no time at all. . . . You know what I ought to do?"

"Yes," she said. "I would not blame you."

"Give me your horse," Conant said.

He took her reins and mounted the black horse, swung around and looked toward the distant east rim of the gorge. She moved back against the bridge and watched him calmly. There was nothing between them. He could shoot her down or ride away. Neither ending would affect his future if he was caught. It was in his hands.

Bloody as hands could be, he thought, but not with a woman's life. Not yet; or ever. Not for the cheap satisfaction of revenge. He had never considered that, even toward the man who sent him to Santa Fe. But some things might be spoken.

"You didn't owe them a damn thing," Conant said.

"That is true," she said.

"The old man won't change," he said. "I don't know about Tony, he acted different to me . . . you notice it?"

"Yes," she said. "He became a man."

"Part of a man," Conant said. "But that was it, eh?"

136

"Yes," she said. "If I live, I will be the woman in my house. My own house."

"Can you handle them now?" he asked.

"Yes," she said proudly. "Because of you."

He laughed softly as the irony of it all touched him at last: the memory of his giving and her taking, how it had changed everything for him on this day. He saw the riders silhouetted on the east rim, come suddenly from nowhere, tiny black figures against the lighting sky.

"There's a lot we could say," he said. "We could jaw all day, but why say it . . . Good-by, Rachel."

"Go with God," she said.

"Not me," Conant said bitterly, moving as he spoke, leading the brown horse. "Not me. . . ."

He put the black to the west rim trail that rose in countless switchbacks and hairpin turns, up and over the receding branches to the west rim and the mountains beyond. There was so much to say, and yet, if he had the time, what could he say? She had tricked him and now he had three hours' start at most, instead of three days, but he could not blame her. Nor was there time to think it all clear, say who was right or wrong. He rode from death for life, and looking back as he made the first turn, watching the riders tip off the east rim and come down the trail, he spoke aloud.

"Not from behind. By God, three days or three hours, you'll not get me from behind."

He rode on as sunrise colored all the land and drove the shadows from the west gorge cliffs and benches, from the crenellated stone castles and the tumbled monuments of time. The black horse responded bravely and the brown, trotting free, led on easy rein. Conant drank from his canteen and felt weariness return, multiplied as the peyote's influence seeped away in sweat and movement. Halfway up the west side, he saw the riders in a similar position far across the widening gorge. He looked down but he could not see her now; the lowest bench cut off river and bridge.

He hunched forward as pain began softly in his stomach and twisted upward through his chest in his arms, the pain of fatigue and hunger and lack of sleep, the exhaustion of a body pushed beyond the limits of any man. Up and around the hairpin turns, past the rock slides, under the towering walls. He topped the last great bench and trotted on the last rough mile to the rim. He would change horses there, ride the brown until it dropped, then bore into the hills between the gorge and railroad tracks; and if he crossed the tracks into the deeper forests, he had a chance. Three hours' start meant fifteen miles if the brown horse could run that far before it dropped. The black, beneath him, was still strong.

"Come on," he said. "Come on, boy!"

He rode fast up the slope, detoured a rubble mound, and saw the west rim outlined clearly. The bullet struck a rock beside him and shrilled away; and Conant dropped against the black's neck and drew the Winchester and looked upward in one movement.

"*Alto!*"

He saw them, five men spread along the rim, showing heads to emphasize the odds. One called again down three hundred yards of rock and cactus, telling him to stop, to give up. The voice was unmistakable, the thick and softly accented throat of the Indian tracker speaking now in an alien English tongue. He had one moment to raise his arm in acceptance or dive into the rocks and prolong it for an hour, until fifty men came from below and finished the surround.

Conant dropped the lead rein and spurred the black

horse. They bounded upward on the faint width of trail and he saw the rubble path that angled upward and reached the rim far to the south. He turned the black horse and felt the big feet slide and dig into the loose shale. He lay over on the river side of his saddle and heard the shout again.

They were playing fair, more than fair, but that was all behind him. Then the black horse faltered as the life was torn from its body. He kicked his boots free and dived as the black fell, and they reached him there, on the rubble slope fifty yards beneath the rim. Really to understand, you must see him as he no longer existed in his world of that time, dead on the rocks in his own land, an ordinary human being caught up in the most ordinary net of shoddy acts.

Ten

THEY WERE ALL VERY TIRED WHEN THEY STOPPED AT
Casper's farm. Men and horses milled beside the creek,
roiled the water, muddied the green grass. The U.S. marshal went up to the house where old Casper was standing
in a circle of his neighbors, face flushed with wine, arms
waving as he spoke. The marshal entered the house and
tipped his hat to Rachel Casper, who stood with her husband beside the table. She spoke first, offering him a chair,
but he refused politely for lack of time.

"I just wanted to tell you," he said. "I'll take care of
it. I can't say what share they'll give you, but it'll be at
least half."

"It does not matter," Rachel said, and her husband
echoed her words.

"No matter, Marshal."

"No," the marshal said, "I don't guess it does. Not

after what you went through, the way you stood up to him. By God—and excuse me, ma'am—but I wish I could say I'da kept on fighting the same way.''

"Sure you would," old Casper said loudly, coming from the yard. "Why, Marshal, you and me are the old breed. I never even thought of giving up . . .''

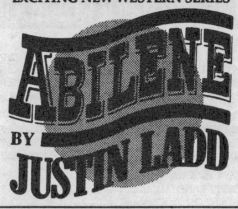